RULE THE AIRWAVES
RULE THE SCHOOL

Published in the UK by Scholastic Children's Books, 2019
Euston House, 24 Eversholt Street, London, NW1 1DB, UK
A division of Scholastic Limited.

London – New York – Toronto – Sydney – Auckland
Mexico City – New Delhi – Hong Kong

SCHOLASTIC and associated logos are trademarks and/or
registered trademarks of Scholastic Inc.

Text © Roman Kemp and Vick Hope, 2019
Cover characters and inside illustrations by Jason Cockcroft, represented by United
Agents © Scholastic, 2019

The right of Roman Kemp and Vick Hope to be identified as the author of this
work has been asserted by them under the Copyright, Designs and Patents Act
1988.

ISBN 978 1407 19692 3

A CIP catalogue record for this book is available from the British Library.

Printed by CPI Group (UK) Ltd, Croydon, CR0 4YY
Papers used by Scholastic Children's Books are made
from wood grown in sustainable forests.

1 3 5 7 9 10 8 6 4 2

www.scholastic.co.uk

LISTEN UP

RULE THE AIRWAVES
RULE THE SCHOOL

ROMAN KEMP & VICK HOPE

In collaboration with Chloe Seager
Illustrated by Jason Cockcroft

THE THEFT

[Intro: *Radio Royalty* jingle (5 secs).]
ARTHUR: "Listen up, Victory Road! It's the night of the school's annual chess tournament and the atmosphere is BUZZING…"

The lone sound of someone's laughter echoed round the empty school hall, making Arthur sit up.

"Yeah … no one's going to believe that," said a familiar voice from behind him.

Grace Best. Of course she would be here early too. She stood in front of Arthur with her arms folded across her chest and a patronizing arch in her eyebrow.

"All right," said Arthur. "It's the night of the school's annual chess tournament and the atmosphere is DEAD AS A GRAVEYARD." He laughed at his own joke, but Grace shook her head in mock-pity, making her big, black curls bounce around her shoulders like a hair advert.

"Well *that's* not going to win you any awards for radio journalism, is it?"

She fake-smiled and walked to a seat at the far side of the hall – as far from Arthur as possible – then set down her bag and pulled out a huge book with a chess piece on the front. *Of course she'd done a ton of research for this,* thought Arthur, *and of course she was thinking about awards in radio journalism already.* Grace was always two steps ahead of everyone else, including Arthur. Even her last name was annoyingly smug.

Well, she wasn't going to get the best coverage tonight – Arthur was. But he seriously needed to find a way to make a chess tournament sound fun. Arthur knew Grace would already have her take on the event worked out, but he didn't plan ahead like that. His style was more off the cuff, so inspiration could come from anywhere and ideas always hit him eventually. Although sometimes, like today, they took a little while.

Arthur gulped. What if inspiration *didn't* hit? What if all he had was some boring, standard coverage of a chess tournament?! Arthur shook his head. He wouldn't let Grace Best get in his head! That was exactly what she wanted – to make him nervous so that *Best of the Best* would beat him and his best mate Kieran's radio show, *Radio Royalty*, in the school ratings this week. Theirs were the two most-listened-to shows at Listen Up, the school's radio station. And no matter how hard Arthur and Kieran tried,

3

Grace was always competing with them for the top spot.

Their styles were quite different. Arthur and Kieran tended to chat with the interviewee and draw them out slowly, whereas Grace was more blunt and straight to the point. But they all desperately wanted the scoop on stuff going on around school.

"Your Highness!" shouted a voice.

"Your Grace!" replied Arthur automatically as he stood up and bowed theatrically to his best mate Kieran, who was standing in the doorway surveying the room like a real king.

This was how they always introduced themselves – in real life and on their show. They fist bumped and sat down next to each other. Arthur felt more relaxed now Kieran was here.

On the other side of the room Grace was trying to read, but the two "kings" whooping in the corner were distracting her. She reached secretively into her bag for one of her mum's puff puffs. OK, so they were delicious, but couldn't her mum ever just give her a Kit-Kat? Her bag was always bulging with huge boxes of Nigerian snacks and it was so embarrassing.

Arthur and Kieran erupted into snorts and Grace finally put down her book. She'd practically become an overnight chess expert, anyway – she even knew all about castling. She

twiddled her thumbs and looked over at the two boys, then quickly away again. *What's it like to have a best mate?* she wondered, with a little pang of jealousy. Grace had friends, but… She sighed. Everyone knew her as "that radio girl". It was kind of like being famous, or that's what she thought. People wanted to hang out with her, but she didn't have any close friends. Arthur and Kieran obviously had a bond – and they obviously had each other's back. Grace wasn't sure if she'd ever find that.

She looked out of the window at the pouring rain. It was unusually rubbish weather, even for winter, and Grace wondered who – apart from her, Arthur and Kieran – was actually going to show up for this. She'd even had doubts about whether she should come, but there was no way she'd let *Radio Royalty* get a possible scoop over *Best of the Best*. As the thoughts turned over in her mind, the doors opened and a surprising number of kids started schlepping in.

With some in twos and some in groups, they noisily filled up the hall. Grace caught Arthur's eye.

"Told you, Bestie, BUZZING!' he shouted, and he did a victory dance. Grace rolled her eyes and the kids still walking in looked between them in amusement; their rivalry was well known around school.

Well, she had to admit it: Arthur was right. The atmosphere *was* buzzing.

As everyone took their seats, the chess-players began filing on to the stage. The first to walk out were the Klimach sisters, Nikita and Misha, instantly recognizable by their long, dark hair and pale skin. They were practically identical and wore similarly determined, narrow-eyed expressions, but Nikita was older than Misha. They'd been winning chess tournaments together since they were really young. Next out was Jordan Baptiste, with his locks and cool shoes. Jordan acted like an old man trapped in a twelve-year-old's body – he was always contemplating the meaning of life. Next came a small, blinking, dark-haired first year called Bea Shaffi. Grace had found her lost in the corridors on a couple of occasions and she seemed like a sweet kid. She was closely followed by Roddy Lyall, who was the headmistress's son, and her spitting image with red hair and freckles. Everyone called Bea a chess prodigy, but Roddy... Well, Ms Lyall entered him for everything, whether he wanted to compete or not. They were the youngest contestants and they both looked petrified.

In the hall, Arthur nudged Kieran and pointed over at Alan, the school caretaker, who had entered from the right hand door by the stage, carrying a large, gleaming trophy.

Their slightly scary headmistress Ms Lyall, who was sitting right at the front with Roddy's little brother and the rest of the contestants' families, got up to introduce the competition. She stood at the front of the stage, right by the trophy.

"Welcome," she boomed, "to the tenth annual Victory Road chess tournament. This year we've got a wealth of talent – old and new – competing, and I wish every contestant the very best of luck. So without further ado, let the games begin!"

She gestured towards the trophy and the hall burst into applause.

Bea's eyes brightened, Roddy fidgeted in his seat, Nikita and Misha's eyes seemed to go even narrower and even Jordan looked full of determination as Alan sat the trophy in the middle of the stage, in all its glory.

Grace braced herself. Maybe this was going to be more interesting than she'd thought.

Or maybe not. One hour later, Grace was

trying to concentrate on the game, but it was hard. None of her books had mentioned that chess was this S L O W.

The first few rounds had been OK. They were quick-fire chess, which meant the opponents had to move every ten seconds. Arthur had been in his element, bopping around yelling, "Ouch, that's gotta hurt!" when a piece got knocked over or, "Ooh, that was below the belt!" and doing dramatic countdowns in the players' ears. At one point, Roddy was so alarmed by him that he accidentally won. The crowd had broken into raucous laughter and Arthur had given a bow. Even Grace had to admit it was funny.

But now they were down to the semi-finals, there were no time limits on the games, which meant the remaining players were really

taking

their

time.

Despite his accidental win, Roddy had been swiftly eliminated in the quick-fire rounds and sat awkwardly on a bench by the side of the stage. So now it was down to Bea and Nikita, and Jordan and Misha. It felt like time was standing still. Grace was *sure* the clock had stopped moving. And by the looks of things, they still had quite a long game to get through. People were starting to shuffle in their seats and stare out the window. Even Arthur seemed to have run out of jokes. The only sound was the rain beating on the roof, and the deep rumbling of thunder.

Come on, pay attention, Grace thought to herself. *Radio Royalty* had been outdoing her this evening, but this was her moment. While Arthur and Kieran had been focusing on the individual games, Grace had been uncovering the history between the players.

The elusive Klimach sisters were supposedly

unbeatable; they had *never* lost a game in the school's chess tournament history. But this year was different: they usually played as a team, but tonight they might play against each other.

Bea was an underdog because of her age, but could she become the first person ever to beat the Klimach sisters, and the youngest winner of the chess tournament *ever?*

Or would it be Jordan, who was currently playing the oldest Klimach sister, Nikita. She had beat him to the coveted science prize – had he been practising day and night to ensure his trophy, and his revenge?!

Now that *sounds interesting*, Grace thought to herself with a smile. And she'd wait for exactly the right moment to liven things up.

"Uh-oh, it looks like Jordan's caught between a rook and a hard place!" Arthur quipped, attempting to break the silence. "A, um, rook and a … hard place…" he repeated, desperately trying to rally the audience. But it was no use. One girl at the back was actually snoring. Kieran patted him on the back.

"Tough crowd, mate," he whispered. "Tough crowd."

He was about to break out his ace card, i.e. singing "Killer Queen" – a song his dad unfortunately sang in the shower a lot – when Grace interrupted.

"It certainly looks like Jordan's running out of options," she spoke into her headset, which was so much fancier than Arthur and Kieran's old-fashioned mic. "Will he use his knight to block Nikita's queen, or maybe … use the ever-slippery castling trick?"

Arthur stuck out his bottom lip and blew in frustration. He wished he knew what castling was. He wished he knew what the pieces were called. The little ones were pawns, right? Or were they bishops? Did Grace always have to know *everything*?!

"It seems tensions are once again running high between the two science prize finalists," Grace went on. "Of course, Nikita won that round, with her impressive purple glitter volcano just pipping his invisible ink to the post. Will Jordan let her claim this year's science trophy *and* the chess trophy?"

At that, the whole hall seemed to gasp at the same time, and everyone sat up straighter in their chairs. There was what could only be described as a gleeful flicker in Nikita's eyes, and Jordan narrowed his back at her. They both looked hungrily towards the trophy. Arthur cursed Grace... She had made the game *so* much more interesting. The room was suddenly alive again. Even the sleeping girl at the back had woken up.

Arthur had to up his game.

"Looks like Jordan has accepted the challenge,"

he said. "He rides his horse into battle."

Both he and Kieran neighed and the room laughed. *Excellent.*

"Jordan uses his *knight,*" said Grace, looking at Arthur pointedly, "to protect himself. But will it be enough?"

The commentary seemed to have spurred Nikita and Jordan on. They were both leaning right over the board and making moves at double speed.

"OUCH! Looks like Nikita's emotions got the better of her," yelled Arthur.

"She didn't think that through carefully," said Grace.

"Now her QUEEN IS SLAIN!"

"With Nikita's queen down, an irreplaceable hole is left in her defence!"

"Oh, oh, my boy is GUNNING for her!"

"Will Jordan take advantage of this new opportunity?"

"Have the tables turned?"

"Nikita still has more of her pieces, but Jordan is undeniably gaining ground…"

"He's closing in! He has her *surrounded!*"

Just then, there was an almighty crack of thunder, which sounded like it came from right above their heads. Everyone in the school hall looked up at the ceiling and, right at that moment, the lights went out.

The hall fell into total darkness.

For a moment, no one said anything.

Then whispering began.

Someone shrieked.

Ms Lyall yelled out, "CALM DOWN," but her deep, booming voice only spooked everyone more. The hall broke into scared laughter.

In all the confusion Grace's headset fell somewhere by her feet. Arthur was tapping his mic. The power was out. How were they going to explain this to their listeners? This coverage was live!

Arthur shuddered. He didn't like the dark. Grace reached into her bag for a comforting puff puff.

The sound of a scraping chair echoed in the hall. Then … footsteps.

"NOBODY MOVE," called Ms Lyall. "WHOEVER THAT IS, SIT DOWN. FOR HEALTH AND SAFETY REASONS IT IS IMPERATIVE YOU ALL REMAIN SEATED."

But the footsteps continued. Someone was disobeying Ms Lyall. Who would *dare?*

"I COMMAND YOU SIT DOWN THIS INSTANT."

The footsteps stopped and an eerie silence descended.

Grace was on her second puff puff by now and had managed to accidentally tread on her pencil case. Arthur's eyes still hadn't adjusted to the dark at all and he was starting to feel really spooked. What on earth was going on?

Finally, the lights came back on with a *pop*, leaving everyone looking around and blinking at each other like moles coming up from underground.

Ms Lyall breathed a sigh of relief. "Thank you, Alan," she said to the caretaker, who was standing by the fuse box. Alan was a man of few words and simply nodded in response then disappeared back into the shadows with his mop. Arthur would bet money he probably spent more time with his mop than with any human beings. Not that he ever seemed to be actually cleaning with it.

Murmurs rippled around the hall again as everyone regained their vision and their bearings. The chess contestants glanced at one another, shuffling in their seats. You could tell everyone was baffled about what had happened and whether they should continue.

"Is everyone all right?" Ms Lyall asked. She seemed thrown too, which was unusual for her. "Shall we, uh, pick up where we left off?"

"Errr, miss?" piped up Bea.

"What is it, Bea? Are you hurt?"

"No, miss, it's not that." Her eyes were full of fear. She pointed towards the centre of the stage. "The trophy. It's gone."

AN UNFORTUNATE CIRCUMSTANCE

[Intro: *Best of the Best* jingle (7 secs).]

GRACE: "Listen up, Victory Road! This is *Best of the Best* and it's time for your weekly news update. The top story this Friday is last night's chess tournament. After a highly suspicious power outage, it appears the coveted Victory Road chess trophy was stolen … right in the middle of the match and right under everyone's noses. Investigations are ongoing."

Perfect, thought Grace, having practised out loud three times already. It was the morning after the "incident", as Ms Lyall had referred to it, and Grace was preparing her special news segment all about last night.

When the lights had come back on, it had quickly become clear that Bea was right: the trophy *was* missing. Hushed, frantic whispers had rippled around the hall. A *thief?* At Victory Road? Who would do such a thing?

Ms Lyall had turned a startling shade of puce. She demanded that no one would be leaving until everyone's bags had been searched – until Mr Pathak had coughed politely and reminded her that they couldn't keep any students in the building beyond six o'clock, and it was already five minutes to. At that, Ms Lyall's puce cheeks had darkened to a deep purple.

"FINE," she had bellowed. "But make no mistake … whether it be tonight, or tomorrow, or next week, or *years from now* when you're bogged down by never-ending utility bills and complaining about taxes, I WILL find that trophy. I won't rest until the thief is brought to JUSTICE!"

The word "justice" echoed dramatically around the hall. Bea wrapped her arms around herself. Nikita inhaled sharply and Jordan, who was normally so calm, raised his eyebrows. Even Roddy, Ms Lyall's son, whimpered.

"Mark my words … whoever you are, we will catch you."

Grace had looked at Arthur. Arthur had looked back at Grace. And in that moment she'd known he was thinking the same as her: this was the most exciting thing to happen at Victory Road in years. Whoever *did* catch the thief would have the scoop of the century.

Grace shivered with the thought of a real thief being out there, and at the thought of being the one to find them. She could see it now ... announcing that she and she alone had tracked down the villain. Students would have to listen to *Best of the Best* to find out who it was – she could do teasers and countdowns to reel them in for the big moment. Her numbers would *skyrocket*... She might even break the school record! And the cherry on top of it all? She would finally beat *Radio Royalty* for good.

Grace's mum popped her head around the door. "What are you doing, *ada*? You're going to be late."

Grace smiled. Her mum always slipped into Nigerian when she was feeling affectionate (or when she was angry). She called her "ada" which meant "daughter". Grace liked it when they were at home, but when they were in public or her mum called it out loudly at the school gates it made her cringe. Especially if someone asked her what it meant or tried to repeat it.

23

Sometimes she wished her mum would just call her "honey" or something when they were outside the house.

"I'm just practising a news segment," Grace answered. "About the theft last night."

"I still can't believe it." Her mum came and sat down on the bed and began playing with Grace's hair. Grace's mum would spend hours doing her hair for her and Grace loved it. It was one thing that was just hers and her mum's. Not involving her brothers, Lucas or Nathan. Not even her dad. "Do you have any ideas yet about who did it?"

"I've got few thoughts," said Grace.

Her dad popped his head around Grace's door. "What's your theory?" he asked. "Where are you going to start investigating? Have you done your research?"

He put his arm round her mum and they smiled at each other. Her dad was round-faced with a short, smart haircut. He was always wearing grey suits and ties because of his job at the council. Her mum had huge hair just like Grace's and worked in television, so was usually in far more relaxed clothes with lots of bright colours.

"Oh, is Grace going to catch the Victory Road thief all by herself?" Nathan laughed as he walked past her door.

Grace fumed. Her brothers never took her or her show seriously.

"Of course she is! Our Grace has a nose for these things – killer instincts!" Her dad beamed at her. "Now, Grace, record your segment quickly and let's get going. Nathan and Lucas, leave your sister in peace."

Everyone left the room and Grace breathed a sigh of relief. She loved her family but sometimes her parents' high expectations and her brothers' relentless teasing was a lot to take.

Nathan and Lucas weren't going to stop her, though; if anything they spurred her on. She'd show them, and Arthur too.

Bring it on, Arthur, she thought, putting on her mic headset to pre-record her news piece. She turned it on and … nothing. The green light wasn't coming on.

"Come on," she whispered, repeatedly pressing the button. Still nothing.

Her heart sank.

Last night, in all the commotion, she'd taken off her headset before munching on some puff puffs. In the dark she'd stood on something that had crunched underneath her shoe. She'd thought it was just her pencil case, but what if…

"No!" she cried out, shaking it. "No, no, no! Come on, please!"

A tear slid down her cheek as she accepted it was actually broken. How was she going to get the scoop now?

★

Arthur had been eager to get into school early that morning. Usually he stumbled down to the car as late as possible, hair unbrushed and clothes pulled on haphazardly, but today he'd been waiting downstairs early for his dad. He'd stood turning his trusty mic, which he affectionately called Mikey, in his hands. Today was a big day. The story of the century had presented itself and *he* was going to be the one to reveal it.

When his dad had seen him waiting there, he'd nearly fallen over in shock.

"Who are you? What have you done with my son?" his dad joked as he began loading up the car.

Arthur had been deep in the middle of a daydream where he caught the thief, found the trophy, and recorded the whole thing. His and Kieran's ratings had obviously shot so high Ms Lyall had declared she was going to award a new school trophy for "journalistic integrity" and give it to him and Kieran. As he'd been handed the award he said to Grace, "See, I *did* win an award for journalism, Bestie."

Suddenly Arthur realized his dad was looking at him. "Huh?" he said absent-mindedly.

"He's away with the fairies, dreaming about his radio," said Arthur's mum from the door. "But then, what do you expect with the example you set?" she eyed the guitars Arthur's dad was loading into the car. Much like Arthur and his sister Kirsty, Arthur's mum wasn't impressed with his dad's band, "Lad Dadz". She often teased Arthur's dad by saying it was a silly dream that he should have given up on years ago. Especially since her career as a lawyer had started taking off.

"She loves it really. What woman can resist a man with a guitar?" Arthur's dad said, winking. Arthur's mum giggled. Arthur shuddered.

Arthur's dad drove them to school every morning and usually Arthur loved chatting with his dad, but today he'd been too focused on getting the scoop to concentrate on anything else. Anyway, Kirsty – always the A-star student – had chattered away about her prep for Oxford University the entire time. Kirsty was only fourteen, but in her words, "It was never too early to start preparing." She and Grace Best would probably get on like a house on fire.

Arthur knew exactly who he was going to interview first: Nikita, because *she'd* been losing when the trophy was stolen. He knew exactly where to find her at lunchtime too – actually, he had the whole day planned out…

After his dad dropped them off, Kirsty waved him goodbye and he went instantly to find Kieran to discuss tactics. Until Ms Lyall's stern voice blared out over the school speakers.

"Would Arthur McLean please report to my

office immediately. Thank you."

Arthur stopped walking abruptly. Everyone in the corridor turned to look at him. Someone even went, "Oooooh."

Well, that derailed his plans. What did Ms Lyall want?

He walked as slowly as possible, his heart speeding in his chest. Had someone already found the trophy? It would be OK as long as it wasn't Grace – how humiliating would that be? It would be her fastest victory yet… *Radio Royalty* pipped to the post in less than twenty-four hours.

When he finally arrived and Ms Lyall ushered him inside her office, he spotted Bestie across the room and his heart sank. Were his worst fears about to be confirmed? But then, she didn't look like someone who'd just discovered the biggest scoop of the year. She looked like Kieran did when he'd accidentally dropped his chicken nuggets on the floor.

Arthur sat down opposite Ms Lyall's huge, intimidating, ornately carved desk, waiting for the news. And it was more devastating than he'd imagined.

"So, from now on, you will be sharing a microphone," Ms Lyall concluded.

Arthur's mouth was hanging down towards the floor. "You're kidding."

"I never kid, Mr McLean," returned Ms Lyall coolly.

Grace winced. When she'd finally stopped mourning the loss of her headset and pulled herself together, she'd come up with a plan of action. Step one was visiting Ms Lyall's office immediately. She'd felt better when Ms Lyall promised to help her, but her hopes had been promptly squashed when helping her turned out to mean sharing Arthur McLean's microphone.

Arthur slumped in the chair beside Grace, his

bum practically on the floor. She understood
that he was upset, but could he never just sit up
properly?

"But … it's mine!" said Arthur, hugging the
mic close to his chest.

"That microphone is school property, Mr McLean. A concept that seems to be lost on the students of Victory Road." Ms Lyall sighed and glanced pointedly at empty space in the trophy cabinet by her desk. "So far I've allowed you to commandeer it because no one else needed it, but it doesn't belong to you."

"Yeah, I mean, I know, *technically* but…" Arthur leaned in towards Ms Lyall, rocking his chair forwards. "Have you seen Harry Potter, miss?"

"Have I…?"

"You know the bit where Harry gets his wand, and as soon as he holds it in his hand he feels it? And that old bloke, can't remember his name, he says 'The wand chooses the wizard, Mr Potter,' in that creepy voice…"

Arthur waited for Ms Lyall to laugh, but she remained stony faced.

"OK, not a HP fan, I get it. Me neither.

33

Anyway, you catch my drift – that's like me and Mikey, here." He waved the mic around. "He feels at home in my hand."

Grace's lip wobbled. That was how she felt about *her* mic.

"You don't really want to use this old thing, do you, Bestie? What about your fancy pants headset?"

Grace's throat felt tight. She looked at the floor. She couldn't bring herself to say out loud that it was broken, and that she couldn't ask her parents for another one. It had been a very special birthday present. Her parents had only given it to her because they knew how much her radio show meant to her – and on the solemn promise that she would take care of it. They'd be *so* disappointed in her if they found out.

"Mr McLean, this is not up for discussion. You'll be sharing the microphone and that's

34

that. You two need to work together from now on and I don't want to hear another word about it. I've got far more important things to be thinking about, like finding this thief."

"But—" Arthur wanted to tell Ms Lyall he was determined to find the thief, too, and he was way less likely to do that with Grace Best around.

"Not another word, Mr McLean. Now, get back to lessons, the pair of you."

Arthur opened his mouth to protest again, but the look on Ms Lyall's face made him think again. Plus, Grace did look properly upset. He didn't want to make her cry or anything. Partially because he'd have no idea what to do if she did. How did one comfort a sobbing girl? Probably slapping her on the back, like he did when Kieran came last in Mario Kart, wouldn't cut it.

He nodded. "All right, come on Bestie."

He got up and Grace sloped after him. When they were outside in the corridor he turned to face her.

"So, obviously me and Kieran are using it this lunchtime, but—"

"Obviously?" She arched her eyebrow.

"Well, we already have interviews planned…"

"*I* was going to do interviews too," said Grace, widening her feet, almost taking on a warrior stance.

Unbelievable! Just when he was beginning to feel sorry for her. He was sharing his mic with her and *she* was telling *him* when he could use it? He squared his shoulders.

"Who were you going to interview first?" Grace asked.

"I'm not telling y—"

"Nikita, of course. She's the only logical starting point. She was losing when the trophy was stolen."

Arthur bristled. Why was Grace *always* right?

"Seeing as we're starting in the same place, let's both find Nikita and take turns using the mic. Ten minutes each should be enough. Meet you at her classroom at one o'clock?"

She was bossy, too. Arthur would have loved to argue with her but her constant rightness made it hard.

"See you then," he said. Grace nodded and began to walk to her lessons while Arthur leaned back against some lockers. Agh, how was this happening? The biggest story to break at Victory Road since he'd started here, and he was sharing a mic and interview slots with Grace Best, his biggest rival?! This *so* wasn't how he expected the day to go.

"Bestie!" he called after her. "Nothing's changed, all right? This doesn't mean we're working together."

"No, it means I'm going to take you down

using your own mic, Arthur!" she called back.

Oh, that really was below the belt. Now he was more determined than ever to get the scoop before she did.

THE OBVIOUS SUSPECT

When Arthur and Kieran arrived at the classroom where Nikita spent her lunchtimes (it was where they kept the chessboards, and kids sat in corners doing sudokus or extra-extra-extra-extra maths) Grace was already there.

"Told you we should have come earlier," said Arthur.

Kieran shrugged. "There was pudding." Nothing, in Kieran's view, was ever more important than pudding. Arthur sometimes wondered if he happened to be kidnapped by masked swordsmen, or eaten by a shark, whether Kieran would finish his pudding before coming to his aid.

"I didn't even know this room was here," he said, changing the subject.

"That's because it's for smart people," said Kieran.

"Hey, I'm smart!" cried Arthur.

"Kidding mate, 'course you are."

Arthur laughed along with Kieran, but deep down he felt a little swoop of panic in his belly. Arthur had always been creative and full of ideas. He was excellent at English and art and languages … but sometimes, when he was trying to divide a sum or solve an equation, he would stare at the page longer than some of his classmates seemed to. The numbers would look like a random, jumbled swirl and it took him ages to make sense of them. Actually, sometimes he *never* made sense of them.

Arthur tried not to let on to Kieran that he found some things difficult. Kieran wouldn't understand, because he was basically pretty good at everything. He wasn't top of the class, like Grace or Arthur's brainy older sister Kirsty, but he was a solid all-rounder and there weren't any subjects he seemed to struggle with, whereas Arthur often had to ask Kirsty to explain things to him when he got home.

"Hi, Kieran," said Petra, a girl in their maths class, peeking out from behind her Sudoku and waving.

"Hey," replied Kieran.

Petra blushed and raised the sudoku back in

front of her face.

That was the other thing Kieran seemed to breeze through – talking to girls. They *loved* him. Probably because he was annoyingly charming, good-looking and had a tan even in winter. He was half-Spanish, so all he had to do was say, "*Buenos dias,*" and some group of girls in a corner would break into giggles. Arthur had been fine at talking to girls too, until last year when they stopped feeling like pals and more like a hair-flicking, nice-smelling alien species.

Arthur watched Grace, making emphatic hand gestures and maintaining intense eye contact as she interviewed Nikita, who looked weary. They were sitting opposite each other at a desk and Nikita was leaning further and further back as Grace leaned closer and closer towards her. Grace was practically whacking her in the face with the microphone. *His* microphone.

"Come on, Kieran," he rallied, "Let's go.

Grace is getting all the good stuff."

They headed over to the two girls. Grace was so deep into the interview she didn't even notice them. Or maybe she did but chose to ignore them.

Arthur coughed. Grace still didn't look up.

"Grace, I think that's your ten minutes," he interjected.

"I've got two left."

At that Nikita's eyes seemed to glaze over, as if those two minutes were stretching out endlessly ahead of her.

"So, to summarize, you have no knowledge of the current location of the chess trophy."

Arthur's eyebrows flew up his forehead. He had to hand it to Grace, she was bold. She sounded more like a detective than a radio presenter!

"For the last time, no," sighed Nikita.

"You have no idea how the slime got on stage?"

Arthur and Kieran frowned at each other. *Slime? What slime?!*

"I don't know anything about slime," said Nikita.

"What about jelly?" Grace prodded. "You and your sister both like jelly, don't you?"

Nikita's face paled.

"You like this particular kind of lime jelly *so*

much that you have it in your packed lunch *every single day*. Correct?" Grace smiled smugly.

"You seem to know more about the contents of my packed lunch than I do," Nikita quipped.

"Not *really* a direct answer to my question, but all right," said Grace. "And I suppose you don't know anything about the glove found at the crime scene, either. Correct?"

Nikita shrugged.

"For the benefit of listeners, Ms Klimach is shrugging noncommittally."

"I am not *noncommittal*," hissed Nikita. "I don't know anything about slime! Or gloves!"

Kieran elbowed Arthur. "Gloves?" he mouthed.

"Play it cool," Arthur whispered, although inside he was panicking. They didn't know anything about any of these clues that had supposedly been discovered! His head was whirring. Clearly Grace was one step ahead, but he wasn't going to let her know that.

"So you've really never seen … *this*?!" said Grace, whipping out a white glove from inside her pocket and dangling it in front of Nikita's nose. She scanned Nikita's face closely but Nikita's expression remained unchanged.

"*Well*?" Grace prodded.

"No. I've never seen it."

Grace's lips tightened. The gloves were her ace card. She had hoped to throw Nikita completely off-balance and get a reaction out of her, but it hadn't worked. She needed to change tack.

"Oh no?" she continued. "Into science aren't you, Nikita? Winner of the science prize, with your glorious purple glitter volcano?"

Even through her exasperation, Nikita's eyes shone. You could tell she was super proud. "Yes." She nodded.

"So these aren't the kind of gloves used in a

science lab?" Grace went on.

Nikita peered at the glove, then back at Grace. "It depends on the experiment," she said finally.

A smile spread across Grace's face and Arthur knew she'd got what she wanted. It was nothing solid, but she'd planted enough seeds to make for an interesting interview. Theoretically, they *were* the kind of gloves Nikita might have been carrying around with her, or would have easy access to. If they were found at the scene of the crime then that was strong evidence against her.

"Thank you, Nikita. This has been most enlightening."

"Can I go now?"

Grace smiled again. "Yes, you can go."

Nikita leapt out of her chair at lightning speed.

"Wait, wait!" Arthur cut in. "Nikita, you said we could interview you too?"

Nikita's shoulders sagged. After the grilling

47

from Grace, the poor girl looked like she needed a nap. Her hair was bedraggled and Arthur could've sworn she'd aged about a decade since the interview began. She looked like his Great Aunt Mildred before her morning coffee.

"All right, fine," Nikita spat bitterly, sitting back down.

Arthur looked at Grace, giving her the cue to disappear. But she just raised her eyebrows at him, leaned back and settled in for the show. She even opened a lunchbox full of those delicious-looking snacks she always carried around with her. What were they called? Muff muffs or something? He noticed Kieran's eyes widen like saucers as he smelled them.

Arthur clicked his fingers in Kieran's face. "Focus, Kieran!" This was serious. Grace had got leads – *actual leads* – and they had a big fat nothing.

But as soon as they began, Arthur knew it was

a bad interview. He always got a feeling within the first five minutes whether an interview was going to go well or not, and if it got off on the wrong foot he always found it hard to recover. This was one of the worst starts ever.

Firstly Grace was watching them, which made him feel uncomfortable. Secondly, Nikita was knackered. Thirdly, in the pressure to get more information than Grace he had completely forgotten his usual style – there was none of the spirit and laughs that made *Radio Royalty* so great. Kieran tried to banter with him a couple of times, but Arthur missed his cues because he was too determined to needle Nikita. When he finally did remember to make a joke, Nikita just narrowed her hawk-like eyes at him in response. All Arthur managed to get out of her were some reluctant instructions on how to make a science project volcano (baking soda and vinegar, but she wouldn't give up any of her "secret winning

49

ingredients".) As if *that* was useful!

Arthur thanked his lucky stars that it was pre-recorded, not live. The interview wasn't even usable! He watched her run out the door feeling unbearably disappointed in himself. His and Kieran's chances of getting the scoop and winning the top spot in the Listen Up ratings this week were slipping away. And Grace had all kinds of clues that they didn't.

Arthur buried his head in his hands. "We have to interview her again. Do it better," he said.

"Yeah, good plan mate," replied Kieran.

Grace smirked. "I mean, if you want to waste time on a dead end," she remarked, packing up her bag and getting ready to go.

"What's *that* supposed to mean?"

"Yeah, what about the glove?" said Kieran. "And the lime jelly? It all adds up."

"*And* the fact she was losing when the trophy was stolen," added Arthur.

"And she's all … shady-like!" Kieran narrowed his eyes in an impression of Nikita.

"She's obviously the culprit, you said so yourself!" Arthur cried.

"Yeah, *obviously*. Because in all good crime novels, it's always the *obvious* choice," Grace snorted.

Kieran knitted his eyebrows together. "This isn't a novel, this is classroom 3B at Victory Road." He looked around him, as if to reassure himself Hercule Poirot wasn't lurking under the table.

"All right, boys," Grace said as she hitched her rucksack on to her shoulder. "You go chasing after that second interview with Nikita. I'll be making actual progress."

"So where are *you* going?" Arthur asked, his irritation rising.

Grace laughed. "As if I'd tell *you*."

Arthur smiled. Finally, he was one step ahead

of her! "See, that's the thing about sharing equipment, Bestie," he said, folding his arms. "You kinda don't have a choice – you can't ditch us."

Arthur thought about how much he would have preferred to interview Nikita without Grace there and how he'd been stuck with her. Now she was trying to go solo without them? Er, no way!

Grace turned on her heel and flounced out of the room. "Watch me. And don't you dare follow me!"

Arthur and Kieran looked at each other.

And started following.

THE STOOGE

Why oh why oh why did I have to be so cocky? thought Grace as she twiddled her thumbs, waiting for Kieran and Arthur's interview with Misha to be over. If she'd just kept her mouth shut, Arthur and Kieran would still be trying to get their second interview with Nikita! Instead, all the work she'd put in this morning – going back to the assembly hall, visiting Ms Lyall's office for a second time to check what had been found at the scene, convincing her to lend her the glove and even take a bit of slime in a plastic bag – all that research, she'd basically handed to her biggest rivals on a silver platter! She could practically see her dad shaking his head at her. "Arrogance is a roadblock on the highway of wisdom, Grace," he'd say whenever she showed off. It was one of his favourite sayings. Now she wished she'd taken it more seriously.

Grace couldn't *believe* they'd actually followed her. It was like they were on some silly spy mission. She thought she'd heard footsteps behind her in the corridor and turned around once or twice, but they must have hidden, because she hadn't seen them. It was the giggling that gave them away and Kieran's voice whispering, "Ouch, doughnut!" By the time she found them crouching behind some lockers, breathless with laughter and hugging each other, it was too late. They knew exactly where she was headed. On top of it being incredibly annoying, Grace couldn't help feel a little tug in her heart as they rolled around on the floor wheezing. She

didn't think she'd ever had that much fun with a friend. *Ever.* Not even at a birthday party or something, let alone at school.

"I can't *believe* you didn't clock us!" said Arthur, once he'd finally finished laughing. "We were so unsubtle. Kieran tripped over a bin. But, all right, come on, Grace. Why is Nikita's younger sister a more likely culprit than Nikita?" He pointed at the door to classroom 2B, which was where Misha's year group sheltered from the rain at lunch.

Grace bit her lip, wondering how much to tell them. She supposed the game was up now, so she might as well share.

"All right, fine. It couldn't have been Nikita because of her shoes."

Kieran and Arthur looked at each other.

"Her shoes?" Kieran asked. "As in, like, on her feet?"

"Nah, I normally wear my shoes on my

head," Arthur joked.

"You will be if you keep back-talking me like that, McLean," Kieran said with a wink.

Grace smiled. They *were* a funny pair, she had to admit. "On the night of the theft she was wearing heeled lace-up boots," she answered.

"So?" said Arthur.

"*So,* listen to this." Grace fished her phone out of her pocket. She pulled up a recording and hit play. "When the lights went out and my mic fell on the floor, it carried on recording on battery power until I trod on it. It was on the floor so it recorded the thief's footsteps perfectly," she finished breathlessly. Grace was actually excited to share her findings with people, even if it *was* Arthur and Kieran.

The boys leaned towards Grace's phone eagerly, and Kieran held a hand around his ear theatrically. The soft footsteps played. Even having listened to the recording ten times over,

Grace shuddered hearing them again. They were eerily quiet and it was chilling to hear the thief in action. From the looks on their faces, she could tell Arthur and Kieran were creeped out too.

"As you can hear, the footsteps are practically silent," Grace went on. "Obviously made by a light, soft shoe, or socks. Not big clompy boots."

Kieran leaned away from the phone. "Couldn't she have taken them off?"

Grace rolled her eyes. Boys knew absolutely nothing about fashion. "In the thirty seconds that the lights were off? She'd have had a tough job even getting *one* of them unlaced."

Arthur and Kieran nodded, intrigued. "You're right," cried Arthur. "Bestie, that's genius! You just properly eliminated a suspect!"

Grace couldn't help but feel sunshine glowing in her tummy. She was quite pleased with her deductive skills – and it was nice to have Arthur being kind to her for once. He seemed to have surprised himself, too, because then he coughed and made his voice all gruff and deep.

"Urrrm, yeah, anyway."

He coughed again. "Back to Misha. What are we thinking? She did her sister's bidding? Is she Nikita's stooge?"

"They've been an unstoppable chess duo since primary school," said Grace. "They *could* be in it together. Or Misha could have done it on her sister's behalf without her knowing. Either way, she's a prime suspect."

Kieran and Arthur nodded with her, and for a split-second Grace almost forgot they were the competition. Until Arthur said,

"Well, seeing as you went first with Nikita, we'll be going first with Misha. Thanks for the info, Bestie!" And with that, he strolled into the classroom. Kieran shrugged at her apologetically and followed him in. Grace took a deep breath, wishing she had something to throw at Arthur's head.

It was four minutes until their interview was up. Grace was trying to calm herself, think logically and prepare for her own interview. She toyed with the glove. It was white, wrist-length and fairly large. She had to return it to Ms Lyall's office before the end of lunch, so she wanted to remember every detail of it. She stared at it closely, as if it might have the thief's name written on it somewhere.

It was hard to concentrate, though, with Arthur and Kieran's boisterous chatter going on in the background. Grace listened in for a moment and smiled with satisfaction when she realized they were *completely* off topic.

"I swear, I am – I'm allergic to marshmallows!" bellowed Kieran.

"Kieran, no one is allergic to *marshmallows*."

Arthur's face was red from spluttering.

"Well *I* am!"

"No, you're not!"

"I am, Arthur, I swear!"

It went on and on like this. *What a waste of their ten minutes,* thought Grace with a shake of her head.

"It's probably the gelatin," said Misha. "It's in lots of snacks. I studied this for a project."

"Ah, are you a scientist too? Did you enter the science prize?" asked Arthur, referring to Nikita's win.

"No, Nikita's the scientist."

"Do *you* know the secret to her winning volcano?" He winked.

She shrugged. "I know to make a volcano you add vinegar to baking powder. That's about it. As I said, Nikita's the scientist." She looked back at Kieran. "So, can you eat jelly?"

"No, I'm allergic to that too," said Kieran

proudly, as if he'd won some sort of certificate.

"It's definitely the gelatin," concluded Misha.

"Woah, woah!" Kieran held up his hands. "So what else is gelatin in?"

"Mate, you're going to have to learn. Your mum isn't going to make your packed lunch for ever," said Arthur.

"My mum doesn't make my packed lunch," Kieran sulked.

"Sure, man, sure."

"Don't worry," said Misha. "I thought I was badly allergic to silver for a long time. But it turns out it was actually nickel. Most silver jewellery isn't pure silver, it's likely to have some nickel in it."

Arthur and Kieran both went silent. *Please say they hadn't figured it out…*

"Silver, like … the chess trophy?" Arthur asked hesitantly.

"Yes, exactly," said Misha.

Nooooooo. Grace was *fuming*. They spent *one minute* asking her about the chess tournament, three minutes discussing whether she'd rather give up chess or sandwiches, four minutes talking about the world's strangest allergies (including cockroaches and the smell of fish – that's right, not fish itself, just the *smell)* and then they'd accidentally hit on this pure journalistic gold, with only two minutes to go? It was so unfair!

"So … what happens when you touch silver, then?" asked Kieran lightly.

"Oh, I go very red and blotchy. Terribly blotchy. It's *hideous*."

"And, er, how long does this blotching last?"

"It can be *weeks*."

There was another silence, and Grace could tell that Arthur and Kieran were both trying to subtly peer at Misha's hands.

"I see you looking at my hands," said Misha, holding them up. "And here, OK, for the record, no redness or blotches."

"Unless you were wearing … gloves?" Arthur suggested cheekily.

Misha sighed. "Yes, OK, fine, unless I was wearing gloves."

"Gloves that were your sister's, maybe…" Kieran added.

Misha scowled.

"Well, I think that's all we've got time for," Arthur rounded up. He was *beaming*. "We *had* wondered why someone would wear gloves to steal the trophy, given that Victory Road security isn't exactly the FBI."

"Do we even have security?" asked Kieran.

"Alan the caretaker sometimes chases pigeons away with a broom…"

"Right."

"Anyway, my point is they were never going to get forensics in, were they? So why would someone bother with gloves? But a nickel allergy … that *is* one plausible option. But I suppose there could be *loads* of other theories, too. Hmm. Can you think of any, Kieran?"

"Not off the *top* of my head, mate, but there's probably loads of them."

"Probably loads, yes. Anyway, thanks *so* much for chatting to us, Misha! We hope you enjoyed your time on *Radio Royalty*, we certainly did!"

Misha, who had seemed slightly friendlier than Nikita initially, now looked like the spitting image of her sister. Her eyes were narrowed at the boys and her mouth was a thin, tense line. They had just made her look totally guilty!

Grace was panicking. Their recording with Misha was so much better than hers with Nikita… All *she* had was a suggestion that Nikita had access to the gloves, but the boys were right, why would a thief at Victory Road even *need* gloves? Unless they had a terrible nickel allergy. The theory made perfect sense!

She needed to outdo them and she needed to do it fast.

"Misha, could I just…" she started.

"No!" said Misha. "I've put up with enough interrogation! I've never been so insulted."

"But—" Grace pleaded.

"No. I've had enough of you … pesky radio kids! No more interviews today!"

"*Pesky radio kids*?! This isn't an episode of *Scooby Doo*," said Arthur, and he and Grace wrinkled their noses. Kieran looked oddly pleased.

Misha stormed towards the door, then turned back.

"Oh, and by the way, it couldn't have been me. Look!"

She grabbed the glove from Grace's hand and put it on her own. It was ridiculously large – like, *comically* large – for her hand, which they now all saw was incredibly small.

"Why would I use these gloves? I couldn't do a thing in them!"

As she gestured, the glove went flying off her hand, clearly demonstrating her point. Grace, Arthur and Kieran all looked at the massive glove lying on the floor. Suddenly, their latest theory seemed very unlikely.

Misha stormed out of the room.

"Well, looks like she probably didn't do it, then," said Kieran.

"Who cares?" said Arthur. "The interview was brilliant! We're going to top the ratings with that one. Then we'll find out who actually *did* do it and smash the ratings again next week as well!"

Kieran and Arthur high-fived.

Not if I find out first, fumed Grace. She was raring to go. No time with Misha meant she had to move on to her next interview *fast*.

"Where to next?" Kieran asked.

"Bea Shaffi," said Grace, at the same time Arthur said, "Jordan Baptiste."

"*Bea Shaffi?*" Arthur mocked. "The tiny one with big, round eyes who wouldn't say boo to a goose?"

"Don't underestimate her just because she's small and cute," said Grace. "She's what's known as a dark horse."

Arthur waved his hand dismissively. "Oh, you and your crime novels. Sometimes things are obvious for a reason. *Obviously*, it doesn't look like it was Nikita or Misha, so *obviously*, the next logical conclusion is Jordan Baptiste. He was the only one still in the game. The only who still had something to lose."

"Plus he's a bit mysterious," added Kieran.

Grace really didn't think it was Jordan. She had a gut feeling about Bea and in good journalism you should always go with your gut. "Look, no offence to your theory, but we're going to Bea next. End of."

But Arthur wasn't budging. "No, Jordan's next. End of."

Grace folded her arms. "Look, you've already wrecked one interview for me…"

"*We've* wrecked an interview for *you?! You* ruined *ours!*"

Grace bit her lip. She supposed putting Nikita under fire *had* somewhat put her on the defensive for Arthur and Kieran's interview. But then Arthur and Kieran's jokey, conversational style had drawn something out of Misha she'd never intended to share, which meant her interview didn't happen at all! This arrangement clearly wasn't working for anyone.

"Look, let's just split up," Grace concluded. "You go to Jordan. I'll go to Bea. We'll swap the mic halfway through lunchtime tomorrow. Deal?"

"Deal!" Arthur cried with relief. He reached

his hand out to Grace at lightning speed and she shook it.

"But Ms Lyall said…" started Kieran.

"Forget what Ms Lyall said, mate." Arthur put his hand on Kieran's shoulder. "Working together is an epic fail."

"I guess," said Kieran. He smiled apologetically at Grace. "See you, then, Grace."

"See you," she answered.

And with that they went their separate ways.

THE DARK HORSE

[Kitchen sound effects. Cue presenter.]

GRACE: "Welcome back to *Best of the Best* as we continue our sizzling special! I'm joined by Bea Shaffi, who's cooking up a storm. Take us through what you're rustling up today, Bea?"

BEA: "Well … I, um, it's a fruit salad so, I cut up this banana."

GRACE: "I see, do go on."

BEA: "And then this apple."

GRACE: "Uh-huh, fascinating…"

Grace spent the evening plotting how she was going to talk to Bea. She was *sure* Bea was hiding something. When the trophy went missing, Bea had been the one to point it out, and then sat there looking fearful and wide-eyed. It was all a little *too* convenient. A little *too* innocent. Grace knew what it was like to be underestimated and she knew what it was like to be overlooked. But Grace hadn't overlooked Bea.

The problem was, both *Best of the Best* and *Radio Royalty* had aired their interviews on Listen Up and the hallways were buzzing with talk of the theft and Nikita and Misha. And actually, *Radio Royalty*'s interview wasn't doing better than Grace's was, as she'd feared. People were interested in both of the sisters being "in it together", so wanted to hear from each of them. Ratings of both shows were soaring!

In one way it was brilliant – Grace hadn't had this many listeners since Mr Pathak's boyfriend proposed to him at the school play and Grace had recorded the whole thing. (Arthur had been really annoyed about that one. Ha.) It was exactly what Grace wanted, except obviously she, Arthur and Kieran knew the sisters didn't actually do it. It would surely only be a matter of time before everyone realized the holes in the theory... They'd need to find new leads, and fast, if they wanted to keep their ratings high and figure out who did it.

But, this all meant that the entire chess crew was avoiding Grace (and probably Arthur and Kieran too) like the plague. Jordan Baptiste was more elusive than ever. Bea Shaffi had seen Grace in the hallway and hidden behind a much larger student. Roddy Lyall had turned bright red and walked the other way. No one wanted to be the next person pushed under the spotlight.

But last night at home, Grace had suddenly had a brainwave. Her brothers had been helping her mum make dinner, which involved Lucas flinging a piece of tomato at Nathan and Grace wondering if they would ever stop acting like babies, and that was when it hit her.

"Cooking!" she'd shouted. "Yes, thank you!"

Bea Shaffi's lunchtime slot was different to Grace's because she was a first year. When Grace was on lunch, Bea would be in cookery class. Grace could pretend to do a cookery segment! Ingenious!

Sure, Grace had never done a cookery show before and the first years only ever made fruit salads and cupcakes, so it would hardly be *MasterChef*, but that was beside the point.

When Bea saw Grace enter the classroom, microphone in hand, she'd looked like she wanted to sink into the floor. *Ha,* thought Grace, *nowhere to hide now.*

To make it convincing, Grace had spent ten minutes chatting to other first years about their choice of fruit which, clearly, had been whatever was going in the school canteen that morning as most of the students had forgotten to bring ingredients from home. Grace didn't know how much longer she could pretend to be interested in apples.

When she finally reached her suspect, Bea instinctively picked up a banana as if to defend herself with it.

"I didn't do it," she said.

"Do what?" asked Grace. "Oh! The *trophy!*" She laughed falsely. "No! Bea, no. I'm here for the bananas. Now, tell me, how do you chop yours?"

Bea seemed to relax then, which was a good start. She put down the defensive banana. But three minutes later, after having to talk to a whole class before reaching Bea, Grace was nearly out of time and all she had was the dullest cooking show ever recorded. Arthur and Kieran would be here to collect the mic soon. She needed to act fast!

"So then I squeeze the lemons…"

"Yeah, that's great, Bea. So, er … tell me about … where you might *eat* this fruit salad? In the field, perhaps? In the library, doing a spot of homework?"

"Um, yeah maybe," Bea replied.

"Or, perhaps you'll take it with you to … chess practice?"

At the word "chess", Bea's eyes glinted with fear. *There it is!* Grace thought. No one looks that scared when they're innocent! But as soon as she spotted the telltale vulnerability, it disappeared. Bea stared at her lemons.

"I don't practise chess," she said. "I'm just naturally good at it. My mum makes me play it but I don't even care. Chess is…" she swallowed. "Chess is lame."

Grace frowned. "What?"

"Chess is *lame*," she repeated.

"But… you've won two national competitions for the under elevens. One when you were only eight, against students much older than you. You were the youngest player in the Victory Road tournament. You're awesome at it," said Grace.

Bea shrugged. "I'm all right."

Grace was lost for words. Something was off – this just wasn't adding up. Instantly she knew she'd been right to follow her gut here.

A group of girls on the next cooking station burst into a fit of giggles, and Bea's eyes darted towards them then back down to her salad. Her long, dark hair fell in front of her face and she hid behind it.

Grace turned and looked at the girls. One of them had been pointing at Bea but stopped as soon as Grace saw her. They were huddled together, holding hands and laughing. Except this wasn't the warm, open laughter of familiarity and friendship, like between Kieran and Arthur, that made her stomach ache. This laughter had a sting to it; it came from the kind of fun built on making someone else miserable.

Suddenly it all clicked into place. Bea was obviously embarrassed because those girls were making fun of her.

Grace looked at Bea with a new-found sympathy. She wondered if she'd even lost the chess tournament on purpose. She'd beaten students better than Nikita and Jordan before… People didn't use the word "prodigy" for nothing! Did she lose on purpose, then feel too upset to see the trophy go to someone else? Or did she steal it to show off to those girls … to prove she really did think chess was "lame"?

Just like that Grace saw a motive. It was a sad one and her heart ached for this talented girl who was holding herself back just to fit in. But no matter how sorry she felt for Bea, stealing wasn't OK.

Something caught her eye in the doorway. It was Arthur jumping around, waving a… Was that a walking stick? And was Kieran wearing a fake beard?! Grace blinked.

"TIME!" Arthur mouthed at her. She turned back to Bea.

"Thanks for chatting with me, Bea." She glanced at the group of girls on the other station. "Remember, no one can make you feel inferior without your consent."

That was another of her dad's favourite sayings. Bea gave her a small smile and Grace headed over to Arthur and Kieran. Arthur was now frantically tapping his wrist.

"All right, all right," Grace said as she approached them. "Calm down, grandpa."

Arthur doffed his old man cap in greeting.

"Why are you dressed like that?" she asked.

"Same reason you've developed a sudden interest in cookery," Arthur said. "We're going *undercover*."

"I know Kieran's wearing a fake beard but I *can* still recognize you. Sorry." Grace smirked.

"*Ha-ha,* very funny," Arthur replied. "We're doing a segment on the school drama club."

Grace nodded. Of course. Jordan was a member of the drama club.

Reluctantly, she handed over the mic. But as she watched Old Man Arthur and Old Man Kieran retreat towards the school arts centre, she longed to grab it back. After all the progress she'd made, she was itching to continue investigating and record her findings! She sighed as she looked around the empty hallway wondering what to do next.

Just then, she noticed a flash of ginger hair whip around the corner. A piece of paper fluttered to the floor. Had someone been standing there?

"Hello?" she called out. "Excuse me, you dropped something!"

She followed them around the corner but the person had disappeared. The corridor was deserted. She looked down at the piece of paper in her hands and frowned. It was a sheet of music.

Lyall, read the name at the top.

Why was Roddy Lyall hanging around by the first year classrooms?

As the bell rang and Bea's class came piling out, Grace instinctively hid behind a corner. The students filed along the hall, walking and talking in groups. Some went to the vending machine, some headed straight off for lunch. And as the crowds cleared only one girl remained. She was shuffling from side to side, checking her watch.

It was Bea.

And she was *obviously* waiting for someone.

Grace looked at the sheet of paper in her hands and felt her journalistic spidey senses tingling. The plot had thickened! Roddy and Bea weren't friends – they weren't even in the same year – so why would they be meeting at lunchtime? Now she was even *more* sure that Bea was up to something, and Roddy was clearly involved somehow. Grace began formulating a new plan... She was going to prove Bea and Roddy did it and tell the world on *Best of the Best!*

THE ONE WITH EVERYTHING TO LOSE

[Intro: *Radio Royalty* jingle (5 secs).]

ARTHUR: "Listen Up, Victory Road! We're in today's rehearsals for the upcoming introspective, thought-provoking production of 'Seaweed, Be Weed', and the cast are delving into exactly why they feel channelling seaweed is the perfect vehicle to tell a story of love and loss…"

"Shhh!" hissed a girl from the floor. "Seaweed doesn't talk! Seaweed doesn't *think*."

Arthur and Kieran nodded and pretended to lie down. They would finish the segment later. As soon as the girl closed her eyes they sat back up again.

"How long do you think he has to keep lying on the floor – sorry, channeling seaweed?" whispered Kieran, pointing at Jordan, who was laid flat across the other side of the room.

"Not sure," Arthur whispered back.

Kieran shrugged and opened a chocolate mousse, dipping into it with a spoon. Arthur had no idea where he kept all the snacks that seemed to appear out of nowhere. Or the cutlery, for that matter. He hoped it wasn't in his pants.

When the boys had arrived at drama club, Mr Pathak welcomed them in and commended them on their fancy dress efforts.

"Everyone," he announced. "Arthur and

Kieran will be joining us today. They're recording a *Radio Royalty* segment on the upcoming play. Isn't that exciting!"

An excited titter broke out amongst the club; they were all clearly excited to be on Listen Up. Although Kieran's fake beard did stick out like a sore thumb, next to the sea of entirely black outfits. He removed it quickly.

"Right, let's get started," said Mr Pathak, continuing regardless. He smiled at Arthur. Mr Pathak was one of Arthur's favourite teachers. Well, he was *everyone's* favourite teacher. He taught English but ran several clubs for students in his own free time, adamant that everyone should have the opportunity to pursue what they were passionate about. Arthur always thought that if everyone had half as much time for other people as Mr Pathak did then the world would be a much better place.

They had spent the first ten minutes of drama

club lying on the floor, pretending they were at the bottom of the ocean. This was definitely *not* how Arthur imagined drama club. He thought it would be all stage combat and yelling, "To be, or NOT to be!" while holding a sword. This felt more like sitting around sombrely in a room full of goths.

"When does the … acting begin?" whispered Kieran.

"I'm starting to think that's not the point of drama club," whispered Arthur.

"Right." Kieran paused. "What *is* the point of drama club?"

Before Arthur could answer Mr Pathak clapped his hands together. "Right, everyone, stand up," he called.

"Finally!"

Everyone else slowly raised themselves from the ground.

"And now …" announced Mr Pathak, "you

are trees. Swaying slowly in the wind."

Everyone closed their eyes again and started rocking back and forth like zombies. Kieran's face fell. He looked at Arthur with desperate eyes.

Arthur agreed. They weren't going to find out anything this way!

"Come on," he whispered, nodding his head towards tree-Jordan.

They began swaying towards him.

"Joooordaaaaan,"

Kieran murmured, waving his arms around in what Arthur supposed was an attempt to be the wind.

Jordan continued swaying with his eyes closed. Man, he was *really* into being a tree.

"Joooordaaaaaan," Arthur hissed, more firmly this time. He held the mic towards Jordan. "Tell ussss, what do you enjoy most about draaama cluuub?"

Jordan was quiet for a moment, and Arthur wondered if he'd even heard them speak. But then he answered.

"Yours is a question with many answers," he said cryptically.

"Care to venture one?" Arthur pressed.

Jordan was silent again. Eventually he said, "The peace and quiet for self-reflection."

Arthur ignored the hint and carried on.

"And what are you reflecting on? Hopes? Dreams? Ambitions? …*Regrets*?"

Jordan breathed in, and out, in, and out. He swayed gently.

"You don't fool me, Arthur McLean," he whispered, and Arthur felt quite unsettled by the use of his last name. "Unlike these simpletons, I know you're not here for a segment on drama club. But sadly … I don't have the answers you seek."

This was like talking to a wise old owl in an ancient book who only spoke in riddles. If only they could find a way to subtly—

"So did you do it?" asked Kieran.

Or they could just get straight to the point. Typical Kieran! Arthur widened his eyes at him and he shrugged.

Jordan opened one eye. "Ah, Kieran Summers," he stated, as if only just noticing Kieran was there too. "You have a young and inquisitive mind. Thank you for your direct and open candour. The act of theft would be …

beneath me," he uttered coolly. "I'm on a higher spiritual and philosophical plane."

Kieran looked totally baffled.

"I'm afraid that's all I've got time for today, boys." Jordan closed his eyes again. "Good luck on your journey of discovery."

"*Young mind*?" hissed Kieran as they swayed away from Jordan. "We're the same age!"

"I don't know, I think Jordan's been about sixty since he was born," whispered Arthur.

Kieran shook his head. "Strange boy. Something's off."

Arthur nodded. He didn't believe for a second that Jordan was "above" the theft. This "higher plane" rubbish was all total nonsense. He'd seen the look in Jordan's eyes when he'd been losing to Nikita and when Grace had mentioned him losing the science prize. He'd also seen the hunger when it looked as if Jordan might win. He'd wanted that trophy. He wanted it *badly*.

Arthur had no doubt that when the lights went out that night, Jordan had ensured his victory. He just had to prove it.

But getting any more information about Jordan was difficult. Half the drama club seemed too wrapped up in "getting in touch with their emotions" to speak to them properly. And the more chatty students seemed to know little more about Jordan than they did! Arthur and Kieran would start by asking a few general questions to get people talking, then slip in a casual mention of Jordan, but the responses they got back were mostly "not sure," "great hair," "he's mainly at the back of the class," or "we've never really spoken, but I like his shoes."

They *had* managed to find out that Jordan was sometimes responsible for the paints and glue for set-building. Kieran had punched the air when they found that out. Potentially the glue could have been the slime that was found on the stage! The slime was one thing that had been puzzling Arthur and now they had a potential explanation. It was a good start … but it still wasn't enough. If they didn't find anything else then they had no leads to follow up next.

"He's an elusive one, isn't he?" commented Arthur, after their fourth failed attempt to glean information about him.

"He's a slippery fish, all right," Kieran agreed.

Drama club was nearly over and they were hardly further along than when they started. Arthur was starting to panic. He wondered how Grace's investigations were going and whether there'd been any developments on Bea. Maybe him and Kieran should have gone with her after all. Bea, though… She just seemed so sweet. And he was certain he was on the right track with Jordan, even if he was a tough cookie to crack… But what if there really was nothing to crack? Maybe he was just the well-dressed boy at the back of the class who spent time quietly reflecting and really *was* too wise and moral to steal anything! Arthur shook his head. Competing with Grace was making him question his instincts. He definitely wasn't going to get anything else out of these drama students, anyway.

"How's it going, boys?" asked Mr Pathak in a loud stage whisper. Some of the drama students were still really involved in being inanimate objects.

"OK, thanks, Mr P," answered Arthur, but really he felt a bit deflated.

"Oh dear." Mr Pathak smiled. "Didn't get what you wanted?"

How did some teachers just know how you were feeling? Mr Pathak always seemed to sense when to leave you alone, or when you wanted to talk about something, or when you needed extra help. He should teach other teachers that skill, thought Arthur. Some were completely clueless.

"Not quite," he admitted.

"Some of the drama students are a little bit…" Mr Pathak paused to choose his words carefully. "Well, they're just very involved in the club. Perhaps I could be of service?" He smiled.

Arthur doubted Mr Pathak would be able to give them what they wanted, but he was being so nice and they had two minutes left. It couldn't hurt, right?

They switched on the mic and started asking him questions. About how he started the club, what they normally do and the play they were working on. It was always fun chatting with Mr P.

"And it's so much bigger now than when we started," said Mr Pathak. "We've nearly doubled in size over the past few months! Which is amazing! Except we can't all use the studio at the same time any more. There was a point when I thought we'd have to call off the play because I just couldn't manage the rehearsals and extra sessions by myself. But thankfully, Alan's stepped in."

Arthur frowned. "Alan? The caretaker?" He thought of their quiet, reclusive caretaker. Somehow Alan and drama rehearsals didn't seem to go together.

"Yes, only this morning, actually. When Jordan told me I—"

"When *Jordan* told you?!" Arthur's mouth dropped open. He looked at Kieran.

"Yes, I believe asking him was Jordan's brainwave. And what a great idea. The show *will* go on, as they say!" Mr Pathak clapped his hands together.

Arthur's mind was whirring. *Jordan* had convinced *Alan*, the man who barely bothered to change the school's lightbulbs, to help out with *drama club?* Alan, who also happened to have been in charge of the lights at the chess tournament?!

It looked like they'd found exactly what they needed after all.

"Thanks so much, Mr P, you've been amazingly helpful," burbled Arthur. "Good luck with the play. Come on, Kieran, let's go!"

Kieran looked confused but followed Arthur out of the studio. Arthur would explain everything to him once they got outside. They needed to make a new plan of action ASAP. He smiled to himself. He'd been right about Jordan all along. Thank goodness he'd followed his own instincts instead of listening to Grace… Something was afoot with Jordan and the caretaker, he just knew it!

FOLLOWING BEA

[Chart music sound bed.]
GRACE: Aaaand concluding the Top Ten
Favourite School Dinners with the expert help
of the dinner ladies… Aaaaat five: turkey
twizzlers have really stood the test of time;
they've been a firm favourite for a decade…
What're we saying, ladies? In at four: potato
smileys … always brighten up their maker's
day. Up one place to three: it's fishcakes, no
one really knows whether it's fish or cake…"

Amelia Spooner-Popperwell Birtwhistle-
Hughes put her hand on Grace's shoulder. "I
think it's *so* great, you interviewing the dinner

ladies," she said. "How marvellously fascinating. The *beating heart* of Victory Road."

Grace smiled. "Um, thanks."

It was the day after she'd seen Roddy waiting for Bea. She'd only been interviewing the dinner ladies to get a good view of Bea eating lunch, but talking to them had been super interesting.

"Come and sit with us?" asked Amelia.

"Uh…" Grace hesitated.

It wasn't that she didn't like Amelia, as such. It was more that Amelia was the sort of girl who *collected* friends. She was one of those straight A students who seemed to be involved in every extra-curricular activity going. She was also one of the poshest girls in school and she could be quite … well, snobby. She only befriended people who she deemed "talented" enough to be in her little group. She'd been trying to befriend Grace since her show's ratings went through the roof last year. Amelia was fun and everything, but Grace couldn't help but remember how she'd never taken an interest in her before *Best of the Best* had taken off.

Still, Amelia's table was right next to Bea's, so today Grace had agreed to join her. She followed Amelia to the left corner of the canteen, half listening to her chat and half keeping an eye on Bea.

Since yesterday, Grace had been doing some digging – she'd had her suspicions about Bea, but some of the evidence had still been nagging at her. If the glove had been too big for Misha, them it was *definitely* too big for Bea. Plus, where on earth did that slime come from? She'd also been doing some basic mathematics. Based on the recording of the footsteps – which she'd obviously replayed a million times by now – it seemed a little far-fetched that Bea would have made it over to the trophy and back to her seat in time before the lights came back on. She'd have to have moved at lightning speed and, well... Bea was academically gifted, for sure, but she wasn't exactly athletic. Grace had been watching her and she could barely coordinate her hand to her mouth as she ate lunch.

But since Grace found out that Bea was in cahoots with Roddy, everything had made a lot more sense. He was knocked out of the competition and sitting on the bench, which meant that he was much closer to the trophy. He would have easily had time to snatch it. Also, a thorough search through his social media profiles last night showed that Roddy had *extraordinarily* large hands for a twelve-year-old boy. Just about perfect for the abandoned glove, Grace would say. Scanning through his photos one could also notice a single, massive change between eleven-year-old Roddy and twelve-year-old Roddy: *hair gel*.

One moment Roddy looked like a short,

young kid with dry, tousled ginger hair. Then over the summer holiday he transformed into a gangly lad on the edge of becoming a teenager, with slicked-back hair that looked as if it had been dunked in a vat of grease. Perhaps the slime wasn't slime after all… Perhaps it was hair gel! Grace was still confident that Bea was the brains behind the operation, but Roddy had obviously helped her commit the crime. Now she just had to find out why.

As Amelia and her friends chatted about Amelia's new show dog, Winston, and all the tricks he could do (apparently, he could walk a tightrope), Grace craned her neck to get a view of Bea at the next table.

Strangely, Bea appeared to be sitting with the girls who'd been making fun of her yesterday. She was pushing her food around her plate and not joining in the conversation. The other girls were acting like she wasn't at the table at

all. Why, Grace wondered, would you sit with people who were so mean? But then Grace remembered why she'd sometimes sat with Amelia, or with other groups, before deciding she was better off on her own. Sometimes just being around people felt like the obvious answer to loneliness. It had taken Grace a few years to work out that being around the *wrong* people was the loneliest place of all.

Grace narrowed her eyes. Every so often Bea would check her watch, which meant that she was either counting the minutes until she could get away from these girls or … she had somewhere to be. And, perhaps, someone to meet. Grace bet she knew who that *someone* was.

"…And he can nearly juggle with satsumas…" Amelia went on.

(This Grace *had* to see. Maybe she'd do a segment on dog shows after all this was over.)

Suddenly, Bea stood up. All the other girls at

her table stopped talking and stared at her. One of the girls, the one who'd been pointing at her in class earlier, was saying something. Grace leaned closer, away from Amelia's dog talk, to try and overhear.

"...you didn't say," the girl said.

"Oh, I guess I ... forgot," finished Bea quietly.

"Well, when do you think you'll be done? I didn't even know you played an instrument."

Grace couldn't hear Bea's response. The girl was being really mean, but she was right to be suspicious. Bea *didn't* play an instrument. Grace had done enough research about her to know that. But whatever response Bea gave seemed to satisfy her, because she nodded as if she was bored of talking to Bea and turned back to the rest of the group. Bea slunk off quietly.

It was go time.

Grace shoved the rest of her disgusting school pie in her mouth. "Shorry guysh..." she said through a mouthful of pastry. "Got to…" She swallowed. "Go."

Amelia and her friends looked aghast at Grace's table manners.

"Oh!" cried Amelia. "But you've only just sat down!"

"Sorry. Urgent radio business."

"Of course. She's a busy bee this one," she said, looking to one of her friends conspiratorially. She glanced back to Grace. "Off you pop!"

Grace breathed a sigh of relief and hurried after Bea, who was already halfway down the corridor and disappearing into the shadows.

Gosh, Bea's fast, thought Grace, as she tracked Bea across Victory Road. Maybe she was athletic after all – she moved swiftly and silently through the busy corridors, weaving her way in and out of the other students like a snake in the grass. She was small and almost invisible and could slip easily through gaps between people. No one seemed to notice her! *But I notice you*, thought Grace.

Grace felt like a hyena stalking its prey. She was keeping up well enough, too, until ... she crashed straight into her brothers. Great, just great – this was the last thing she needed! They stopped abruptly in the middle of the hall and peered down at her.

"Woah, slow down there, little sis!" said Nathan, raising his hands.

"Yeah, where are you off to in such a hurry?" asked Lucas.

"And why are you all the way over this end of the school?"

"Is it *important radio business?*" said Lucas, putting quotation marks around the words "radio business" with his hands. They looked at each other with knowing smiles.

Grace felt rage bubbling in her stomach. She

clenched her teeth. Her brothers never, ever took her – or *Best of the Best* – seriously. It was really starting to wind her up.

"None of your business," she answered, trying to push past them, but they stood together in an

annoying brother-barrier.

"Let me *GO!*" she shouted. She didn't have

time for this. Why were her brothers so beyond irritating? If they kept her any longer Bea would escape! Only, in her desperation to get away from them, Grace realized she'd called out quite loudly, and everyone in the corridor had heard her.

Everyone, including Bea.

Bea's head, and several others, turned towards her. *No!* Her brothers would give her away! There was only one thing for it. To hide herself, she pulled them into a massive group hug.

Lucas and Nathan went totally rigid as Grace grabbed their arms around her. Everyone in the corridor eventually stopped staring and carried on.

"Um, are you OK, little sis?" Nathan coughed.

"Yeah, what are you doing, urgh," said Lucas. But he didn't break her cover by pushing her away. Both of them just stood rigidly in shock.

When she was sure that Bea wasn't looking, Grace squirmed her way out of their arms.

"Urgh to you too," she said, looking between the gap in their shoulders. In their surprise at being hugged they'd forgotten to block her, but it was too late: Bea had disappeared. Her brothers had totally ruined everything!

She had to think quickly. Where might Bea be going? Bea had mentioned something about an instrument, but Grace had never been musical so she had no idea where to go.

"If I was playing an instrument, where would I do that?" she asked.

"Um, Music Room B?" Nathan offered, pointed her down the corridor. He was clearly so taken aback by being hugged by her that he'd forgotten to be annoying.

Grace started running.

Nathan and Lucas watched after her, stunned, as she legged it up the hall. "Thanks, bros!" she called back, although it was them that'd made her lose Bea in the first place. It was a shot in the dark now that she'd lost her trail, but she just hoped her brothers were right.

When she got to Music Room B everything was crossed: fingers, toes, hair! Her hunch *had* to be right. There were only fifteen more minutes before she had to return the mic to Arthur and Kieran. There just wasn't enough time to be wrong! But as soon as she saw an orchestra gathering through the small, circular window in the door of Music Room B, and Roddy sitting in the front row of the audience, her heart sang with relief.

She scanned the rest of the crowd until she found what she was looking for: a little dark ponytail swaying back and forth in time to the music.

Bea.

She was sitting at the back, far away from Roddy, as if she wasn't there because of him. But Grace knew that she was. She just had to find out *why.*

SUSPICIONS
AND
SEMI-QUAVERS

Grace positioned herself in the back row so that Bea wouldn't spot her, under the guise of recording the weekly recital. Mr Pathak had welcomed her with a big smile.

"Of course, of course!" he said as he ushered her inside. "Record away! It's so lovely to see the most popular kids in school taking such an interest in the music and drama scene!"

Grace flushed guiltily. She *was* interested, of course, although maybe not quite as selflessly as Mr P thought. Still … finding the culprit *was* important to the wellbeing of the school, she reasoned. It just happened to be good for her ratings as well.

Grace had come in halfway through. The first act she saw was a young girl playing three different Ariana Grande songs on a trombone. Grace smiled to herself. She wasn't sure it had quite the same effect, and the girl kept having to pause for breath, but she had to admire her passion for Ariana. Then there was a girl who played the violin so intensely it was like she and her violin were the only two things that existed. She had long hair past her bum and moved her body jerkily as she drew the bow back and forth. The girl was a bit terrifying, actually, but the sounds she made were beautiful. Grace couldn't in a million years have hoped to play half as well. (When Grace played the violin, it sounded more like a cat stuck in a tree). Not for the first time, Grace thought how brilliant it was that the world was full of such different people with incredible talents. She knew she wanted to spend her life discovering them and bringing their stories to the world over the airwaves.

Next up was a young boy playing the piano.

He was the spitting image of Roddy Lyall, only much smaller, and he went a bit red when his turn came. He shuffled nervously towards the piano then turned back, as if too afraid to go through with it, but an old man sitting up front smiled at him and gestured towards the piano encouragingly. Grace guessed it must be his grandfather.

"You can do it, Benjy!" the old man called.

Benjy seemed to take courage from this and carried on. He gave a small wave to Roddy as he sat down at the piano. Clearly this was Roddy's younger brother and must be who Roddy was here to see. She looked down at Roddy's music sheet in her hands; they were obviously a musical family.

Benjy started playing and the whole room was soon captivated. He was actually really good! Grace glanced at his grandfather, who was glowing with pride. But lovely as the music was, she wasn't about to get distracted. She was here to solve a case, after all, and good journalists always kept their heads in the game. She turned to the row behind her and watched Roddy beaming and Bea swaying along smiling. *I see through your act,* she thought.

Then the boy stumbled and the piano made a plinking sound. *Bless him,* thought Grace, *he's so nervous!* Seeing his nerves get the best of him, Mr P stepped in.

"Thank you, ladies and gents, give it up for Benjy Lyall! What a beautiful song!"

The room broke into raucous applause and a few people even whistled. Benjy blushed behind his sheet music and looked over at his granddad, who blew him a kiss and pretended to throw roses at his feet.

When the recital was over, Grace headed straight towards Roddy. He was standing talking to his brother, granddad and Mr Pathak. She planned to interview him about his brother's performance and perhaps wangle something out of him accidentally, like Arthur and Kieran had done with Misha. *Not* that she had anything to learn from Arthur and Kieran, obviously…

"Ah, Grace!" called Mr P as she approached. "Here to interview our budding young musician?" He pushed Benjy in front of her.

"Errr…"

The small boy stared up at her with scared but hopeful eyes. He was incredibly nervous, but clearly honoured at the idea of being interviewed on *Best of the Best*. He was looking at her like she was a celebrity. Grace got that a lot.

"I listen to *Best of the Best* on Listen Up every week!" He smiled.

"Er, thank you." Grace sighed. She couldn't disappoint this sweet kid. She held out the microphone between them.

"So, tell me, about your …" Suddenly Roddy had begun edging away from the group. Her eyes followed him as he sneaked off towards Bea. "… choice of song?"

"It was for my granddad," said Benjy, smiling up at his granddad.

"That's my boy, my, er…" his granddad started.

"Benjy, granddad."

He patted him on the shoulder. "Sorry, Mum says he sometimes forgets things. He used to listen to that song in the war."

"Oh, really? Wow!" exclaimed Grace. Her eyes were still tracking Roddy across the room. He walked up behind Bea and tapped her on the shoulder.

"Yes, on the radio when they could, to help

them feel at home. And to help them feel safe when they were in danger." Benjy spoke like he was repeating words he'd heard a million times over. He was brimming with all the wisdom and stories his granddad had passed down to him.

Grace smiled at the thought of the radio fulfilling such an important role.

"Yes, that was a favourite," chimed Mr Lyall. "That and … *oh now, what was it called…*"

"'*Boogie Woogie Bugle Boy*', Granddad," Benjy helped.

"That's the one!"

He did a little "boogie" and his grandson laughed. Grace stopped thinking about Bea and Roddy for a second. She could only imagine what this man had been through during the Second World War. She made a mental note to listen to *Boogie Woogie Bugle Boy* when she got home.

When Arthur and Kieran arrived to take the mic,

they were surprised to see that Grace appeared to be interviewing ... a random old man?

"What's Grace doing with that old dude?" asked Kieran as they headed over.

Arthur and Kieran were buzzing. Even though Grace had the mic they'd done some more research, trying to dig the dirt on Jordan by asking around people in his form group. Unsurprisingly, their responses about Jordan were largely the same as the drama club's. Despite his huge hair, he had an incredible knack for blending into the background, and everyone described him as "sensible" and "reasonable". *But I see through your high-and-mighty pretence,* thought Arthur.

One of the kids in Jordan's form group had actually seen Jordan *handing an envelope* to Alan, the caretaker. An envelope! The kid said Jordan had explained he'd broken a window with a football and his parents had to pay for the damages. But Arthur doubted Jordan had *ever* kicked a football in his life! No, that envelope was suspicious all right. It smelled to Arthur like *blackmail*. Jordan was blackmailing Alan and forcing him to help out with the drama club, just like he'd blackmailed Alan into helping him steal the trophy. Of that much Arthur was sure. He just needed proof.

They had started out dancing around behind Mr P's head, trying to get Grace's attention and desperate to go and observe Jordan's first rehearsal under the supervision of Alan, but then they started listening to Mr Lyall's stories, too.

Before they knew it, all three of them were swept up in stories of a time gone by. They heard tales of war, peril, sacrifice, loss and heartache … but most importantly tales of friendship, strength and camaraderie. Mr Lyall had put his life on the line on more than one occasion to save his friends – the same friends who had got him through all the most difficult times.

Arthur patted Kieran on the back and Kieran wiped a tear from his eye. Mr Lyall's stories of all his friends, some of who were still with him and some of who weren't, had made Arthur and Kieran think of their own friendship.

By the time Mr Lyall had done talking and Mr P was packing up the instruments, everybody had forgotten why they were originally there. As Mr Lyall and his grandson left, Grace noticed that Bea and Roddy had slipped out and she hadn't even noticed. Arthur and Kieran had even forgotten about nabbing the mic back. The three of them remembered, for a second, that not *everything* was about their ratings.

But it didn't last long.

"What! Is that the time?!" cried Arthur, looking at his phone.

"Nooo!"

There was only ten minutes of lunchtime left –

and *no way* Arthur and Kieran could make it to the arts building in time to spy on Jordan's rehearsal.

"Aw, too bad, guys." Grace smirked.

Arthur scowled. He *had* been feeling emotional, a bit warm even, towards Bestie after hearing those stories. But she was just as annoying as ever! He racked his brains. What could he do to *not* make this a total loss?!

Suddenly he had a brainwave. "Yeah, well, there's still time to catch Bea and Roddy, so I guess we're coming with you," he declared.

Grace snorted. "Don't think so."

"Uh, I *do* think so," said Kieran.

Grace raised an eyebrow. "Good comeback."

Arthur and Kieran looked at each other. Arthur smiled.

"I think you'll find we *are* coming," said Arthur. "Because *you* don't know where they went. But *we* happened to see which direction they were going when we passed them on our way in."

It was a long shot. Arthur prayed she really didn't know where they were; that, finally, he would have something over the always-right and always-one-step-ahead Grace Best!

Grace pressed her lips together. She couldn't believe Arthur had outsmarted her. "Fine," she said, through gritted teeth.

Arthur internally high-fived Kieran. Ha – he'd outsmarted her! And this lunchtime wouldn't be a complete waste of time!

He still trusted his hunch, but if they couldn't investigate Jordan he might as well follow Bestie and make sure she didn't have anything over them.

"Great, we'll lead the way then." Arthur winked at Grace, who glared back at him, and the three of them left the music room together, hot on the trail of Roddy and Bea.

UNDERCOVER MATHS

[Intro: *Radio Royalty* jingle, extra-spooky version (5 secs).]

ARTHUR: [Whispered] "As we tread tentatively through this until now eerily derelict and frankly disturbingly silent wing of Victory Road, you join us on the hunt for an extremely elusive ghost. The ghost of Ms Lyall's sense of humour…"

KIERAN: [Whispered] "Accompany us on our search through dusty lockers, long neglected blackboards, cobwebs larger than your head, classrooms exhibiting the remnants of a maths class cut short… Why? No one knows…"

Arthur and Kieran started the journey joking around, but as they got further and further away from the usual buzz and chatter of Victory Road, their jokes dropped off until they eventually led the way in silence. They were all too tense to speak – who even came to this part of the school? All that was here was the old teacher's offices, before they got moved to a new wing. Everyone knew there were big plans to renovate this building and turn it into something useful, but right now it sat empty. As they crept along dark, barely used corridors, Grace was even more sure of her theory. Why would you come here unless you had something to hide?

As they turned a corner, something made a loud thud. Grace, Arthur and Kieran all jumped out of their skin.

"What was *that?!*" whispered Kieran, clinging to Arthur. Arthur clasped him back.

"Oh, it was just a book." He breathed a sigh

of relief and said, "Doughnut."

"You were the one who jumped on *me*," Arthur defended.

"A likely story," replied Kieran.

Grace wanted to roll her eyes, but she'd frozen in fear, too.

"Are you sure they went this way?" she asked.

"Positive." Kieran was trying to hide it, but his voice was shrill. "OK, does anyone else hear whispers? I swear I can hear whispers…"

"Now who's a doughnut," snorted Arthur.

"You *can't* hear whispers," Grace shot back. "It's all in your head."

In all honestly, she wasn't so sure, but she wasn't about to turn back now.

They continued on, cautiously peering through the doorways of a few empty classrooms until they heard a shuffling coming from one room in particular. They approached, bending low so Bea and Roddy wouldn't see them through the window in the door. Crouching beneath, they slowly, slowly raised themselves up to see. Ugh – the window was so dusty Arthur had to wipe his finger across it. Through the gap in the grime, they could see Roddy and Bea huddled in a corner.

"Yes!" whispered Kieran. "Gotcha!"

Grace's heart was beating double-time. Partly from the spooky building, but also because this was *it*. The big moment when she would be proved right and get to tell the world over Listen Up! It was beyond annoying that Arthur and Kieran were along for the ride, but, hey, at least she could say "I told you so" to Arthur's face when they finally caught Roddy and Bea red-handed.

Grace's breath caught in her chest as they watched the two thieves. They were pulling a big box out of an old, disused locker.

The trophy.

"Aha!" Grace leapt up. Her moment had come! She grabbed the mic from Kieran and crashed through the door, landing with a thud on the old carpet. A cloud of dust puffed up from her feet, it was all very dramatic. "What do you have to say for yourselves, *thieves?!*" she shouted, pointing her finger at Roddy and Bea.

Arthur and Kieran rushed in her behind her, coughing slightly from the dust. Roddy and Bea blinked at them in shock.

"Cat got your tongue, *eh?*" continued Grace. "You were just as quiet when you were stealing the trophy, weren't you?"

Bea and Roddy still didn't say anything, but Roddy was blushing furiously and Bea looked like she might have a heart attack.

"Recognize this?" Grace held up a picture of the white glove. "And have you been using any hair gel lately, Roddy?'

Roddy swept a hand self-consciously through his hair.

"Come on, hand over the trophy," Arthur said softly.

Bea's petrified expression slowly changed to one of confusion. She dragged the box out of the locker and opened it up. Reaching inside, she pulled out...

It was something wooden – a frame with rows of beads hanging across two wooden poles.

"It's an abacus," Bea stated.

There was a moment of silence.

"A ... what?" Kieran frowned.

"An *abacus*. It's helpful for learning simple mathematical concepts," Bea explained. Then she bit her lip. "Sorry, Roddy, not *simple*, I only meant..."

Roddy's redness reached its peak. "It's OK, Bea," he said.

"I'm sorry, but *what's* going on here?" Grace

prodded. By the looks of it, the trophy *wasn't* in the box. But that didn't mean it wasn't here. They were obviously hiding something.

Bea and Roddy looked at each other.

"Bea's been…" started Roddy.

"You don't have to, Roddy," said Bea.

"It's OK, Bea – I can't do this any more." Roddy put his head in his hands. "We have to come clean."

Grace internally rubbed her hands together. *Excellent.* Here it came, the confession she'd been waiting for. She leaned the microphone closer to Roddy.

"I've been meeting Bea in secret for … maths lessons."

Roddy let out an enormous breath. He was staring at his lap like he'd seen a ghost.

Arthur, Kieran and Grace looked at each other.

"Oh yeah, and the rest!" demanded Grace,

but she was already sounding slightly less sure of herself.

"Roddy's telling the truth. That really is what we've been doing," sniffed Bea.

Grace lowered the mic. Was it possible that she had been wrong? That all this time, all Bea and Roddy's secret meetings had just been about … *maths?!*

"Errr … why would you want to keep that a secret, mate?" asked Kieran.

"How would *you* like it if you were so bad at maths that your mum forced you to get extra help from a student in the year *below* you?" said Roddy, looking up from the floor. "She's so determined for me to be good at *everything* that she keeps making me enter competitions!"

Arthur thought about that. He remembered how awful he felt when he didn't get something straight away but everyone else seemed to pick it up easily. Then he imagined how he might feel if he had a mum like Ms Lyall, the competitive headmistress who seemed to prize academic achievements above everything else. He would be so embarrassed if everything he was bad at was under constant scrutiny, rather than what he was good at, like doing *Radio Royalty* with Kieran. He totally understood where Roddy was coming from.

"But what about you, Bea? Were you just keeping Roddy's secret, or do you have a secret of your own to protect?" persisted Grace. She was determined she couldn't be *totally* wrong. If Bea was just keeping Roddy's secret, why was she so jumpy herself?

Bea opened her mouth but, just as she did, the question was answered for her.

"Oh my god, *Bea*," came a cruel voice from the back of the room.

Everyone's heads swung back to the doorway, where a gaggle of girls had appeared as if from nowhere. *When did they get here?* thought Arthur.

Suddenly he realized they were so focused on following Bea and Roddy, they didn't notice that they were being followed themselves. That must have been the whispers Kieran kept hearing!

"I *knew* you didn't really have music practice," said the girl at the front of the clique. Her arms were folded and her mouth was set in a hard line. "You've been doing extra maths – oh my God, that's so sad."

As if on cue, the girls standing behind her laughed automatically. Bea looked like she might burst into tears.

"I don't think it's sad," Roddy mumbled.

"What was that?" asked the ringleader.

"I … I," said Roddy, stumbling over his words. "I said, I *don't* think it's sad. I think being good at maths is cool. I wish I was good at those things." He looked at Bea with genuine admiration.

Yes, Roddy, thought Arthur. It was brave of

Roddy to put himself out there like that, in front of those girls. Roddy had thrown Bea a lifeline, offering her genuine friendship instead of a fake one. He only hoped Bea would take it.

"OK, thanks for your input loser," said the girl. "Come on, Bea. Let's go."

Bea looked like a rabbit caught in headlights. Her eyes flitted between Roddy and the girls. She always seemed small but in this moment she seemed *tiny*, like she wished she would shrink

down and disappear altogether. She stood up slowly.

Arthur's heart felt like it might crack. What if Bea went back to them, and left Roddy sad and alone too? They'd only come here for a scoop and to compete with Bestie, who it turned out was *breathtakingly wrong*, so in a way it was job done. But this just didn't feel right. Arthur took a deep breath.

"I think it's cool too," he said. He balled his hands into fists. This was going to be tough, but Roddy's total honesty had inspired him. "I … well, I sometimes struggle with maths and, believe me, it's not cool at all. It's amazing to be as good at something as Bea is, *and* it's amazing to be brave enough to ask for help when you need it, Roddy."

Everyone was staring at him. It was embarrassing to finally admit he didn't find everything easy, but it felt *good*. He wondered if

Grace, his ultimate enemy, would use it against him, but to his surprise she joined in.

"Yeah," added Grace. "Be proud, Bea, my square root sister. I love maths!" She winked.

"Yeah, you're both *awesome!*" said Kieran, raising his hands in the air.

The mean girl opened her mouth in horror. For the first time, she didn't have a witty, snarky comeback. The most popular kids in school didn't agree with her. If *they* thought Bea's talents were cool then she could hardly disagree. The girls behind her seemed confused too – the leader they looked to for their opinions had been proven wrong. What did that mean?

"Ugh, this is so boring," she finally said to the other girls. "Let's get out of here."

As she turned to go the other girls followed, but more slowly and cautiously this time. One even mouthed "sorry" at Bea as she turned to go. She did look genuinely apologetic. They probably weren't bad kids, thought Arthur, just misguided. School was hard and the urge to fit in sometimes made people do silly things.

"I don't think those girls will be giving you any more trouble, Bea," Arthur commented.

Bea smiled weakly.

But there was one more apology left to make.

"Listen, you two, we're *really* sorry," said Arthur.

"Yeah, our bad," added Kieran. "We totally overstepped."

They both turned to Grace. Arthur knew Grace was incredibly proud, so she'd find this hard, but they really needed to say sorry to Roddy and Bea after embarrassing them like this. Grace bit her lip and Arthur nodded at her encouragingly.

"Yes, we're so sorry," said Grace. She took a deep breath. "It was my fault. I was ... well, I was *wrong*."

Even though Arthur sympathized, given his own confession and feelings laid bare, it was still a *teeny bit* satisfying to hear Bestie admit she'd been wrong.

"Apology accepted," answered Bea.

"Yeah, we're OK," Roddy said with a smile. He and Bea grinned at each other.

Arthur, Kieran and Grace decided it was about time to let Bea and Roddy get down to some serious maths. As they walked back through the dark, dingy hallway towards their afternoon lessons, Arthur wondered if they'd study somewhere out in the open next time, rather than hiding away in this shadowy building as if they were committing a crime. They heard a ripple of laughter from behind them.

"Well… I think Bea's found her first true friend," said Grace.

"I think so too," agreed Kieran.

Arthur glanced at Grace. Was he mistaken

or did she sound a bit down? As if *she* might like a true friend? Arthur was so used to Grace being independent and full of energy, he'd never considered she was anything less than totally happy. But now that he thought about it… who *were* Grace's mates? There was Amelia and that lot, but Amelia only talked to him because he did *Radio Royalty* and he assumed it was the same for Grace. Most people only knew about him because of Listen Up. If he didn't have Kieran he'd probably be really lonely. Was it possible that Bestie was lonely?

"So," Grace said quickly, the usual brightness back in her voice. "I guess we go to Jordan and the caretaker next."

Arthur frowned. "Uh, *we*?" he asked.

"Well, *you* came with *me*," she argued.

"Yeah and *that* turned out well didn't it," he said. "You lead us down a dead end!"

"Oh, because you're so clever?" she mocked.

Arthur shook his head. He didn't need to worry about Bestie. She was fine. She probably only seemed down because her hunch had been wrong. The only thing he had to worry about was beating her... And to do that, he'd need to do more snooping around Jordan and the mysterious caretaker.

THE CARETAKER'S SECRET

[Intro: *Radio Royalty* jingle, overlaid with actor voice: "Lights, camera, action!"]

ARTHUR: "Ladies and gentlemen, it's our pleasure to bring you an exclusive excerpt of the upcoming Victory Road end-of-term production, with a reading from their highly acclaimed opening scene."

KIERAN: "The cast would like to remind you that tickets go on sale next Monday. Over to you guys!"

ACTOR: "Oh, is my home to be clung on a rock or carried on a wave…"

"God, this play is boring," said Arthur. "But to be fair, who knew there was so much to learn about seaweed?"

When he received no response he looked over at Kieran, who was fast asleep with his head back and his tongue lolling out of his mouth.

Arthur burst out laughing, which earned him some serious looks and headshakes from the drama students. He tried to stifle his laughter but Kieran's face was just too funny.

"Wha...?" Kieran snuffled as he startled

awake. "Oh, they're still going then?"

Both boys started silently shaking with laughter.

Last night, after Bea and Roddy's innocence was revealed, Arthur and Kieran were even more resolved to prove Jordan's guilt. He was obviously in league with the enigmatic caretaker, plus he was really the only suspect left. It couldn't have been Nikita because of her shoes: if she'd stolen the trophy, the sounds on the recording would have been much louder and clompier. It couldn't have been Misha because of her nickel allergy, she would have *had* to use gloves to pick up the trophy, and the glove didn't fit her. And it couldn't be Roddy and Bea. The only thing they were hiding was embarrassment over being too bad or too good at maths.

Jordan was the only one left in the game.

Arthur watched Jordan reading from his script: passionately, yet with his usual calm, monotone voice. The drama students were passing the mic around the circle as they took turns to read. Alan the caretaker stood in the corner, watching over proceedings from the shadows with his mop. *Why was he always standing in the shadows?* wondered Arthur. *Did the man ever sit? Or turn lights on? And why did he always carry that mop?* Arthur had never seen Alan *actually mopping*.

Why was he really here? It certainly wasn't because he cared about drama club. He seemed to be in Jordan's pocket, but what was in it for him? Why would he have helped to steal the trophy?

"What did I miss?" whispered a voice from the next row. The smell of something delicious and fried drifted over and Kieran's mouth visibly watered.

Ugh, thought Arthur. Bestie had found them. They'd tried to throw her off the scent by telling her the wrong time for the rehearsal, but she'd obviously not bought it and gone to check the drama noticeboard herself. Arthur wasn't surprised. She was way too smart to be palmed off that easily.

"Nothing," answered Kieran honestly.

Arthur shot him a look. It was true they hadn't found any other clues, but Bestie didn't need to know that! Kieran shrugged in response.

Arthur was surprised to see that Grace didn't have a snotty comeback to this. She just nodded. Clearly having been totally wrong about Roddy and Bea had brought her down a peg or two.

"What are those?" Kieran pointed at her snack. He'd been staring at them the whole time.

"Er, chin chin," she answered quickly, almost as if she was embarrassed. "So what's the next step?" she whispered.

Arthur and Kieran looked at each other. Honestly, they didn't *have* a next step.

"Well I think we should—" started Grace.

"Actually, we've already got a plan worked out, thanks," cut in Arthur. She was just too annoying! Waltzing in here because *her* theory had turned out to be wrong and taking over *their* investigation!

Grace and Kieran blinked at Arthur. "We do?" asked Kieran.

"Yes, *remember,* we discussed it earlier," Arthur replied through gritted teeth.

"So what is it?" asked Grace.

"Um, I'm going to …" Arthur racked his brains. It had to be something big. Something bold. Something that would crack this case once and for all. He'd had a crazy thought last night, but dismissed it. But what if it *could* be done? "… break into the caretaker's office," he finished.

Grace's chin chin, that had been halfway to her mouth, hung in mid-air. Kieran's jaw fell down in shock. He even stopped staring at Grace's snacks.

Arthur gulped.

Grace's eyes opened wide. "You *are*?"

"Yup, sure am. It's … it's cool. No biggie," he stuttered.

He took a deep breath. Why had he said that? *Why why why?* He might as well have said "Oh, I'm just going to dive into a shark pool" or "I'm going to jump out of an aeroplane without a parachute."

In other words, he was *dead*.

Kieran patted him on the back. "It's been nice knowing you, mate," he said.

Arthur started sweating. Sometimes his impulsive ideas lead to total genius, but he had a foreboding sense that this might be the worst idea he'd ever had.

But he'd said it now. There was no backing out. And the more he thought about it, the more he realized that this was the only way he could think of to find any answers.

The caretaker's office was in a little hut on a patch of grass behind the other teachers' rooms. To get there, they'd have to sneak past a whole row of teachers' offices, including Mr Pathak, Ms Grant the eccentric science teacher and even Ms Lyall herself. The three of them stood on the path leading to the hut. It was swarming with adults and danger.

Arthur's legs actually trembled. Was he really going to go through with this?

They'd left the mic back with the drama kids – this was *not* something that should be documented. Jordan was in the middle of his reading and they knew Alan couldn't go back to his office until the rehearsal was over. So they were both safely out of the way ... for now. That meant they had just over twenty minutes

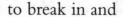

to break in and
look for clues.

Arthur's breath caught in this throat. Break in. He was going to *break in.* To the shady caretaker's office. Who knew what lurked inside? Arthur once heard a rumour that Alan kept a snake in there to deal with the school's mouse problem. The snake had grown big and long from all the mice, and was sizing up its next meal: children. Someone else had told him that Alan had a trapdoor into a dark underground hole, like Ms Trunchbull's Chokey, where he once kept a kid for hours in pitch black because they'd moved his mop.

They were just rumours, Arthur told himself, shaking. Just rumours.

"I heard he's got a massive worm in there," said Kieran.

"You mean snake?" asked Arthur.

"No, no, it was definitely a worm," said Kieran. "So strong it can crush you in one squeeze."

"I heard it was a flesh-eating piranha," added Grace. "And if he finds kids putting gum under the table he shoves their gum-wielding hand into the piranha bowl."

"This is all really comforting, thanks, guys," said Arthur.

"You can do it, mate. And me and Grace will be on guard."

They'd agreed that Kieran would keep watch at the end of the path and Grace would hover outside the hut in case any teachers approached from the other direction. They needed two lookouts for sure, but Arthur couldn't help but think that – out of the three of them – he'd got the raw deal.

"All right, let's go," he breathed. It was now or never. If he hung back any longer he might change his mind and run.

Kieran stayed at the end of the path while Grace and Arthur crouched down and began shuffling along sideways like crabs. They couldn't walk normally because there were no classrooms around this part of the school. If any teachers spotted them here they would definitely have questions.

First they crawled under Mr Pathak's window. Thankfully there were no sounds coming from his room. *He's probably out helping with some club or another,* thought Arthur. *Good old Mr P!* Then they crawled under Ms Grant's window. Ms Grant was delightfully dotty. She was everyone's favourite science teacher because she had mad hair a bit like Albert Einstein and was always doing fun experiments. As they hunched under her window they heard a BOOM! and a BLAST! and a mad cackle.

"What on earth…?" whispered Arthur.

"Doesn't matter. She's too distracted to notice us," answered Grace. "Keep moving."

Arthur nodded and steeled himself. The next window was going to be the toughest to get past. It was Ms Lyall's.

Clip. Clop.

Clip. Clop.

They could hear the sound of her heels smacking against the wooden floor in her office. *Even her feet are stern,* thought Arthur. She was pacing up and down the room, which wasn't a good sign. Ms Lyall paced when she was feeling especially angry. With a sick feeling in his stomach, Arthur realized that Ms Lyall's footsteps were getting louder.

"She's walking towards the window," hissed Grace. "What if she looks down?"

Arthur gulped and looked into Grace's eyes, which were round with fear. But there was no turning back now. "We're just going to have to take that risk."

Grace stared back and took a deep breath. "Keep low," said Arthur.

Slowly as snails and quiet as mice, hardly daring to breathe, Arthur and Grace ducked even lower as they neared Ms Lyall's window. They inched forwards until they were directly under it.

Clip. Clop.

Clip.

Clop.

Ms Lyall's footsteps had stopped.

Arthur and Grace froze. They were so quiet he could hear Grace clench her teeth. Without moving his head, Arthur raised his eyes to look up at Ms Lyall. She was standing *right above them*, looking out over the little garden where the caretaker's hut stood. Just one tilt of her neck downwards and she would see them.

Arthur stopped breathing entirely. He knew

Grace was holding her breath too. Just at that moment, a strong wind blew a bit of Grace's hair in Arthur's face. It tickled *so badly* and he had the strongest impulse to giggle, sneeze and brush it from his nose all at the same time. But he didn't. He had to remain completely still and silent or this whole thing was over.

Clip. Clop. Clip. Clop.

Arthur and Grace both breathed out. Ms Lyall had walked away from the window.

Grace turned and brushed her hair back. "Whoops, sorry," she murmured.

Even in their perilous situation Arthur had to smile.

"Come on," he answered. "We're close."

They kept moving to the end of the building, then crept into the trees and bushes around the edge of the grass. That way they could sneak around the right side of the garden without being seen by anyone who might be looking out of a window, and get into the hut from behind.

Finally, the door to the hut loomed in front of them.

"What if it's locked?" asked Grace.

"Then it's back the way we came," replied Arthur solemnly.

Arthur hovered his fingers over the handle. Grace's lips were moving in silent prayer. If it was locked then this was all for nothing.

The handle clicked and the door creaked opened. Arthur and Grace cheered silently. Instinctively Arthur held his hand up to high-five Grace. "Yes, Bestie!" he whisper-whooped.

Grace gingerly high-fived him back and Arthur remembered they were rivals. He cleared his throat and pulled his hand back. "I'll go in then."

"Right. Err, I'll be here." Grace seemed as awkward about the high five as he did.

Arthur braced himself. It had been no small feat to get here, but they'd done it. He was about to step into Alan's legendary hut. He was about to find some answers.

A HIDDEN TALENT

> [Intro: *Radio Royalty* jingle (5 secs).]
> **ARTHUR:** [OTT voice] "And tonight on our interior design special, we have Alan, going for an extreme 'shabby chic' look, coupled with an overall 'authentic distressed' vibe and a hint of 'hit-by-a-bomb' glamour…"

Arthur's heart raced as he stepped inside the small, dusty hut he'd heard so many stories about. *The hut of legends.*

It was dark and gloomy, and his eyes took a moment to adjust. There was one bare light bulb hanging from the ceiling that was blinking on and off. *Alan never did like changing light bulbs,* Arthur thought to himself. He looked around. The hut was so ... *messy.*

There were piles upon piles of
folders, boxes and cleaning
supplies stacked up in
every corner. Some
of the piles even

reached up to the ceiling! On the back wall hung a massive TV, with what looked like an old-fashioned VCR player attached underneath it, and a pile of videos. The caretaker's old, worn leather armchair sat opposite. *Clearly he spends more time here watching TV than doing any work*, thought Arthur.

At first Arthur trod carefully, just in case the snake was hidden underneath piles of papers. Something made a loud scraping sound and Arthur jumped, but it was just Alan's trusty mop falling over. He propped it back up in its corner. To his enormous relief, it didn't seem like there was any snake. Or Chokey. Or piranha. He started to move more confidently around the room, rooting through the mess. He only had fifteen minutes until Alan's rehearsal was over and, looking at the chaos, he had no idea where to start! But he was determined to find *something*. They couldn't have gone through all the danger to get here for nothing.

He approached a pile of papers and reached to the top, pulling off a big, black binder. The pile wobbled hazardously, swaying from side to side, and a red binder came flying off. Arthur reached forward at lightning speed and caught it in his left hand. *Phew*, he thought, congratulating himself on his lightning-quick reflexes. But just as he was starting to feel smug another one flew towards the floor. Gripping two folders already he had no hands left to catch it and it whacked him hard in the head.

"Ouch!" he called out.

"What's going on in there?" hissed Grace from the door. "Do you need to swap positions?"

"No, I'm fine," snapped Arthur.

As if she could do a better job finding clues in

this mess! he thought. And as if he was going to be on guard while Grace got the scoop! This was *his* theory and it was *his* idea to come here in the first place; Grace was just along for the ride because her own inquiries had failed and because a third pair of eyes was useful for lookout purposes.

Arthur opened the red binder and began flipping through. Electricity bill… Heating bill… Water bill… Nothing. He opened the black binder. Floor plans… Plumbing works… Re-carpeting prices… *Nothing.* He stared around the hut, starting to become alarmed. It would take him *years* to get through each and every one of these piles. What were the chances he was going to stumble on something in *fifteen minutes*?!

OK. Breathe, think, he thought to himself. He would come up with something good; he always did. (Apart from the idea to break into Alan's hut, which admittedly now seemed totally crazy). It was like that on the radio — he'd start interviewing someone and suddenly as he was chatting to them it would all become clear. His take, his angle, the way to draw the best out of them. He looked around the room and spotted a desk next to Alan's armchair.

Aha, he thought. *Of course.* He remembered when he used to go snooping through Kirsty's room, looking for her diary. She'd left a bunch of decoy diaries out in obvious places – under the bookshelf, on the bed. He'd been fooled for months until he'd found her real diary, which was double-padlocked away in a double-padlocked box at the bottom of her wardrobe. What a fool he'd been to start looking through random stuff left out on the floor! If you had something to hide you wouldn't leave it out where everyone could see it, would you?

Arthur eyed the desk, which had drawers up one side. On the top drawer, looped through the handle, was a large, golden, combination padlock.

Bingo.

Five minutes later Arthur wasn't so pleased with himself. He'd tried every combination he could think of (including both Alan and his wife's birthdays, and their anniversary, all of which was circled on a calendar on the wall) and the lock still wouldn't open. Time was slipping away and all he had was a bunch of heating and water bills!

He shook the padlock in frustration. "Argh!"

"Are you OK in there?" Grace whispered.

"Yes, I'm…" Arthur sighed. He was too weary to lie. "No," he answered. "No, I can't open Alan's drawer."

"Just pull it," Grace replied.

She was so *patronizing*.

"It's got a lock on it, *obviously*," Arthur retaliated.

"Do you want help?" asked Grace.

Arthur really did. But he didn't want to admit it.

"I mean, if you *want*," he answered.

The door creaked open and Grace tiptoed inside. Her eyebrows flew up her forehead as she looked around the hut.

"Look at this!" she cried in horror. "How could anyone be so … disorganized?!"

"No time for that," Arthur said, hurrying her. "Come on."

Grace joined him by the desk and he got her up to speed about all the combinations he'd already tried. They both stared at the padlock.

"OK, so not a birthday or anniversary. But

167

there must be some clues in here..." She gestured around wildly. As she did, she hit the remote control for the TV, which had been sitting on the desk, and it went flying into the air. It landed on the floor and the TV turned on.

The sounds of an old ballroom song filled the air. Grace and Arthur's heads snapped towards the screen. A couple in glitzy, bright-blue, matching outfits waltzed across a dance floor. The man dipped the woman down and she threw her head back. Her long curls floated towards the floor and as she came back up her dress twirled around. They looked so elegant as they spun around the room.

"Oh, I've always wanted to cover a dance show!" called Grace. "Live, from Blackpool..." she began commentating. Arthur listened to her, laughing, then looked behind her at the pile of videos sitting underneath the big TV. His breath caught in his throat.

"Grace, look," he pointed. "The videos. They're all the same date."

"18-05-85," Grace read out. They looked at each other, not daring to hope.

"Try it," Grace breathed.

Arthur's hands were shaking as he put the combination into the lock. Eighteen ... five ... eighty-five... As he entered the last digit there was a quiet clicking sound and the lock sprang open.

"Yes!" Grace punched the air. But there was no time for celebrating. In all the time they'd been distracted by the TV, they'd run down to five minutes before they absolutely had to get out of the room. Arthur began rifling through the inside of the drawer.

"You sift, I'll sort," Grace ordered. He methodically combed through the drawer and passed his findings to Grace, who checked if they were anything important.

"Cheque… Birthday card… Valentine's card…"

And then…

"I've found something," said Arthur.

Not just *any* thing. *The* thing. The most important thing they could possibly have come across.

There, lying underneath a pile of envelopes, was a single, large, white glove.

Grace stopped rooting through the papers. "Is that…?" she breathed.

Arthur nodded. He was close to falling over in shock. He couldn't believe his eyes! He picked it up, holding it towards the blinking light bulb to check that it really was part of the same pair. It was — it matched the glove found under the stage exactly. He grabbed Grace by the shoulders and shook her.

"Bestie, it's solved! The case is solved!" he yelled. Arthur started hopping from foot to foot, dancing around with the glove in his hands.

"Kieran's going to go nuts!"

Arthur wondered if Grace would be pleased. After all, it was *his* find, not hers. But then Grace yelled, "Woo-hoooo!!" She stopped looking at the envelope in her hands and started dancing around too. Arthur grinned.

She stopped dancing briefly. "Don't you dare say I told you so," she said before carrying on.

"I wouldn't dare," he laughed.

After they stopped dancing, they both took a moment to soak up the glory. They were elated. Then they looked more closely at the envelope in Grace's hands, which had a post-it note stuck to it.

"*If you don't want anyone to find out, you'll help*

me. J," Grace read.

"J for Jordan! More evidence!'" Arthur was almost giddy. "He *was* blackmailing the caretaker, I *knew* it! This must be the envelope that kid saw Jordan giving Alan! Alan *is* in Jordan's pocket! He got him to steal the trophy!"

"What on earth is the caretaker so keen to hide?" puzzled Grace.

They looked at each other and Arthur opened up the envelope. There were photos inside.

Arthur turned them around in his hands, and what he saw was more of a shock than the glove.

The photos showed two figures alone in the school hall. They were clearly taken after school when it was dark. The two figures were in a close embrace. One of the figures was unmistakably Alan, and the other... Arthur couldn't quite make out *who* the other person was. Whoever they were, they were very thin.

"Who *is* that?" Arthur asked.

Suddenly the truth dawned on Arthur. The other person wasn't a *person* at all…

It was a mop.

"I … I don't believe it," he stammered.

Alan and the mop were doing the same dip as the couple on the ballroom dance show. Arthur and Grace both glanced awkwardly at the mop in the corner of the room.

"He's a … secret ballroom dancer?" breathed Arthur.

Suddenly it all made sense. The caretaker and his mop being totally inseparable. The ballroom videos. The date.

"Grace, google the date on the videos, with the word 'ballroom'."

Grace got out her phone and entered it in. Their screen filled with the images of Alan, the quiet school caretaker, proudly accepting a giant trophy with *Ballroom Dance Champion 85* written across it in sparkly letters.

"Oh my goodness!" Grace breathed. "He's a dance *champion*!"

It was then Arthur noticed something else in the photos, and his heart sank. He squinted to make sure. Alan was wearing the gloves in the pictures. The white, soft, large gloves were *dancing gloves*. Arthur flicked through to the next photo, and the next, all of Alan in different ridiculous poses with his mop. In the second to last photo he was flinging the gloves up in the air with unbounded glee. The very last photo was of Alan (and his mop) leaving the hall.

Arthur pointed to a white mark on the photo. Under the stage, you could clearly see one of the gloves had been abandoned. Exactly where Ms Lyall said it had been found.

"Look at the time stamp," said Arthur. His heart had sunk so low, it felt like it was on the floor.

Grace scanned the picture. "Quarter to six on the nineteenth of October. So?"

Then it dawned on her, too. Realization spread across her face.

"Oh," she said. Arthur nodded grimly.

The nineteenth of October was the night *before* the chess tournament.

"Jordan was blackmailing Alan, but … that glove was there before the thief had even struck. The glove isn't evidence at all," Arthur said.

He couldn't believe it.

"There's no hard evidence that Alan and Jordan had anything more to do with the theft than the rest of the suspects," he concluded.

"You're right. I'm sorry, Arthur," said Grace.

The joy they had both been feeling only five

seconds earlier deflated like a popped balloon. Jordan had definitely been blackmailing the caretaker about his strange, secret dance sessions with a mop and used that to save the school play. But as to the trophy? There was no link at all.

Arthur was crushingly disappointed, but they had to be sensible. Time was ticking and they had to get out of here. "We should leave…" he started, but then they heard a familiar sound.

Clip clop.

Clip clop.

Clip clop.

Arthur and Grace looked at each other, frozen in fear.

"We've got to hide!" said Arthur, and they desperately looked around the room. But the room was so messy there was practically nowhere. It was too late.

"And WHAT is the meaning of THIS?" boomed Ms Lyall, as she towered in the doorway of the caretaker's hut.

A BUMP
IN THE ROAD

ARTHUR: "We interrupt our usual programming to inform you that due to technical difficulties and unforeseen circumstances beyond our control, *Radio Royalty* will not be able to broadcast today. We are doing everything we can to work towards resuming a normal service."

A head peeked around the door of Arthur's bedroom, but Arthur didn't notice until it was too late. When he saw his sister Kirsty standing in the doorway, he scrambled to hide the hairbrush he'd been using as a microphone.

"That's so *sad*," said Kirsty. "I'm sorry you've been reduced to this, little bro."

"I wasn't doing anything." He nudged the hairbrush further under his bed with his foot.

"Sure you weren't," said Kirsty, as she edged into the room and perched cautiously on the bed. *I must really seem pathetic*, thought Arthur, *if Kirsty deigns to enter my bedroom when she usually avoids at all costs due to the, as she calls it, "toxic smell of socks"*.

"But how are you holding up? Mum and Dad are still pretty mad, huh?"

Arthur nodded and looked down. He didn't want to meet Kirsty's eye. It wasn't like he'd never got in trouble before – he had, obviously, – but it was usually unintentional. Maybe he'd accidentally kicked a football into a window, or lost his homework the day before it was due, or woken up Kirsty by doing his radio recordings too loudly. But this was different. His parents had been *called into the school*. He'd never got in this much trouble before and this time there was no excuse. He couldn't exactly say he *accidentally* stumbled into the caretaker's hut and unlocked his private drawer, could he?

Arthur cringed, thinking of him and Grace caught red-handed. Ms Lyall had demanded to see the envelope in Grace's hands. When she'd looked at the photos of Alan dancing with his mop she'd blushed and got even madder, then marched them back over to the main school to start their afternoon lessons without another word. About halfway through double maths, Ms Lyall's stony voice had echoed through the intercom asking Arthur and Grace to report to her office. All eyes had been on him as he'd got up and traipsed out of the classroom. Arthur was used to eyes being on him because of Listen

Up!, but this time it hadn't been a good feeling.

"I heard they went in for a meeting with Ms Lyall." Kirsty went to Victory Road too, so she understood how terrifying that was.

"Yep. She called them in straight away."

Arthur had sat with his parents, opposite Ms Lyall behind her intimidating desk, feeling smaller than ever. *Was Ms Lyall's chair on a raised platform or something?* Arthur had wondered. Because, as she sat there with her hands clasped in front of her, she seemed *HUGE*. Arthur's mum had looked really upset. His dad had looked grave. *Grave.* His dad never stopped laughing unless things were really bad.

"Obviously, I have to treat this situation with utmost seriousness," Ms Lyall had explained. "Harassing the other students. Breaking into a member of staff's office and riffling through their…" She coughed. "*Private possessions.*"

Ms Lyall was clearly thinking of the photos

of Alan dancing with his mop which, even in this situation, still made Arthur want to smirk just a little.

"Well," she went on. "It's unacceptable. I just don't understand what's got into the students." She glanced at the empty trophy case by the wall.

That's so unfair, thought Arthur. *She can't compare me to the Victory Road thief!* He was trying to *catch* the thief, not copy them! Even if he had messed up in the process, his intentions had always been good.

"We understand, Ms Lyall," Arthur's mum had agreed. "Rest assured, there will be consequences at home. Arthur won't be going to the park with his friends this weekend."

"And he won't be coming to see *Lad Dadz* performing, either," Arthur's dad added. "He'll be doing extra homework to catch up on anything he's been neglecting."

Staying inside *all weekend?* Doing *extra homework?* No Kieran? No sunshine, no ice cream, no football? Without so much as a video game to keep him entertained? He never thought being banned from a *Lad Dadz* gig would feel like punishment, but the thought of his whole family going to support his dad without him made him want to cry. This was going to be the worst weekend ever.

"Well, that's good to hear," said Ms Lyall. "But I'm afraid there will have to be consequences at school as well. Unfortunately, I'm going to have to confiscate the school microphone."

Arthur's whole body went cold. Mikey? She was taking Mikey? He looked pleadingly at Ms Lyall and then at his parents. Even Arthur's mum, upset as she was, seemed shocked.

"The microphone? Is that really necessary?" she asked.

"For the time being, I believe it is," Ms Lyall answered.

Arthur's mum and dad looked at each other and finally nodded. Even they wouldn't dare defy Ms Lyall.

They got up to leave and thanked Ms Lyall. Arthur's dad slipped her a *Lad Dadz* flyer. As they left her office, Arthur felt a horrible, empty feeling in his stomach. He saw Grace waiting outside with her parents. It was funny, he'd have thought he'd feel like making a snide remark about her questionable lookout skills, but as they passed each other she gave him a small smile and he returned a quick wink. Even though they were rivals he didn't want her to be upset or blame herself, and it looked like she felt just as sad and small as he did.

"Anyway, I just wanted to check you were OK," Kirsty said, snapping Arthur out of reliving

the trauma. "We're leaving soon to see LD." LD was what Kirsty called *Lad Dadz* because she refused to say their proper name.

Arthur shrugged. He was as all right as he was going to be this weekend. Not only did he hate disappointing his parents and being stuck at home, but it seemed like the Victory Road thief was really going to get away with their crime. He'd never find out what happened now, and he highly doubted the school's own investigations were going to go anywhere.

Kirsty patted him on the shoulder and got up to leave. "All right – bye, little bro. Remember to call Mrs Braverman if you need anything. She's just next door."

"I will. Bye, have fun." Arthur tried not to let his voice wobble.

Once she'd left the room, Arthur sighed. Kirsty had never seen inside the head's office.

She'd never been in trouble. He couldn't even remember the last time his parents had needed to have "a word" with her about anything. How did she find everything so easy? Arthur clearly needed tips because he hated letting his parents down.

He heard the door close downstairs, and his family's voices out on the driveway, laughing as they got in the car. The car doors slammed and they drove away. Arthur threw himself on the bed in frustration.

There must be a way for me to redeem myself, he thought. If only he could find the thief and out them to the world, then everything might not have been in vain… But how? He'd been forbidden from investigating and he didn't have a microphone. Plus, they'd exhausted every single lead anyway!

He racked his brains, going over everything that had led them here. Nikita and Misha had been written off because of Nikita's shoes and the glove not fitting Misha. He frowned. But if the glove wasn't even evidence in the first place, then who was to say that Misha didn't use something else to pick up the trophy? Bea and Roddy had been written off because their secret meetings turned out to just be about maths homework. But, thinking about it, that didn't mean they weren't hiding something else, did it? And then there was Jordan. OK, so, the caretaker's glove had nothing to do with it, but it didn't mean Jordan hadn't stolen the trophy, with or without the caretaker's help. And now they knew he wasn't "above" blackmail, so he probably wasn't "above" theft either.

Arthur sighed. Somehow *all* of the suspects were back in the game. He desperately wanted to talk to Kieran, but he wasn't allowed to. Arthur had never felt so alone and lost. He'd let everyone down and he was further away from solving the case than ever. There was going to be no catching the thief. There was going to be no scoop.

FRESH RESOLVE

Grace was sitting on the floor in her room. She could smell her mum's cooking wafting from downstairs. It was Nigerian Night and egusi soup was on the menu. Usually Grace would be downstairs helping to chop the chilies and onions while her brothers ground the egusi seeds. She could hear Nathan and Lucas flinging things at each other as usual, and her dad telling them to "pipe down". Grace never thought she'd miss ducking underneath flying vegetables, but right now she wished she was downstairs more than anything. Instead, tonight Grace would eat alone in her room.

Tears stung her eyes and her limbs felt heavy. She blinked several times, trying not to cry. Usually Grace was non-stop with homework, helping around the house, reading a book with her dad, watching TV with her brothers, recording a radio segment, preparing what she needed for the following day. But right now she barely had the energy to move...

Grace had *never* been in trouble before. Lucas and Nathan sometimes got reprimanded for various things, but she was a model student!

Grace sniffed. She knew it was wrong to break into Alan's hut and go through his things. She felt awful that they'd exposed something he'd clearly been too embarrassed to share. Her parents had taught her to treat other people how she would like to be treated herself. But they had also taught her to work hard and never let anything get in the way of her dreams and ambitions. So what was she supposed to do – let the thief get away? Lose the scoop?!

Yes, in this case, she guessed. Grace sighed. It seemed like growing up was full of grey areas and tough calls. She had only been following her dreams and ambitions, but this time it felt like she'd made the wrong choice.

She cringed, remembering the moment her parents had found out about her mic.

"I blame myself. I've let things go too far with Listen Up!" Ms Lyall had been saying to her mum and dad. "I've always been aware of the rivalry between *Best of the Best* and *Radio Royalty*, of course. I know it's something of a popularity contest around school." Grace hadn't been in a position to defend herself, so she'd had to kept quiet, but she knew the radio show wasn't a popularity contest. She cared about her show and the popularity was something that happened by accident. Now that she knew Arthur and Kieran, she knew that it was the same for them, too. Ms Lyall had them all wrong.

"I'll be keeping a closer eye on them going forwards and I'll have to temporarily confiscate the microphone," Ms Lyall had continued.

"Don't worry," her mum had said. "We'll put it away for at least a week."

"I was referring to the school microphone," Ms Lyall explained.

"Oh, but Grace uses her own." Grace had looked back at him, and in that moment she'd known she had to confess. She'd been saving pocket money ever since she broke her mic,

in the hopes she'd buy a new one and never have to tell them what had happened, but she'd have to keep saving for at least another six months to even get close. It was time to come clean.

"I broke my mic, Dad," she murmured. "I've been using the school one. I'm so sorry. I stepped on it. I didn't want to tell you because I knew how disappointed you'd be. But it was an accident."

Grace saw the hurt in her parents' faces and looked at her shoes, her eyes blurring with tears. For the rest of the meeting her parents had been quiet, mainly nodding along with what Ms Lyall was saying. Grace had stayed silent.

She never, ever wanted to get called into Ms Lyall's office again. She wondered how Arthur's meeting had gone, and wondered if he was out there feeling as bad as she was right now. She hoped not. She wouldn't wish this on her worst enemy … which she supposed Arthur was.

Where had they all gone so utterly wrong in this investigation? Grace had never been so completely wrong about anything before. She was used to having all the answers. How had she added up a bunch of clues and come out with a big, fat zero? Ugh! They had obviously missed something somewhere along the way that was really important.

They, Grace thought to herself. She supposed she meant *she.* She had never *really* been working with Arthur and Kieran. Although towards the end, it kind of felt like… She shook her head.

There was a soft knock at her door.

"Come in," she called.

It was her dad.

"I've brought you your egusi soup," he said. He laid it on her desk. It smelled really, really good. Comforting, like home.

"Thank you," Grace said quietly. She expected

her dad to put down the soup and go, but instead he sat down in her desk chair.

"What are you up to in here?" he asked.

"Nothing," she shrugged.

"That's not like you," he said.

"Well…" Grace tried to keep her voice from wobbling. "I'm not feeling like myself."

Her dad sighed. "Grace, my love, we're not angry with you for breaking your mic. It's a shame, but we know it was an accident. We're more sad that you hid it from us. And we're not *really* angry with you about the investigation either."

"You're not?" Grace blinked. The weight inside her started to lift, just a little.

"No. I mean, *yes,* obviously." Her dad stumbled. "Officially we are *very angry.* You're a smart girl, Grace, and you know you crossed a line. But we're also, unofficially, just a little bit proud of you." He winked.

"Really?" Grace gasped.

"*Unofficially,* remember." He tapped his nose, smiling. "We raised you to go after what you want. And I don't think I'll ever forget those pictures of old Alan dancing with a mop." He laughed to himself, shaking his head. Alan had been there when Grace's dad was at Victory Road about a million years ago.

"Just don't go quite so far again, OK? We know your radio show is important to you, but there are limits."

"Don't worry, Dad," Grace assured him. "The investigation is over. No more catching the thief. No more broadcasting the scoop on *Best of the Best*."

Her dad nearly fell out of the chair. "What?!" he said, his eyes almost popping out of his head. "No, Grace, no. I never said that!"

"But..." Grace started.

"Look, don't go breaking into any more

teachers' offices. But you can't give up now!"

"But Ms Lyall said…"

"*Pfft*," her dad snorted. "*Ms Lyall said.* You and that boy… What's his name? The one with the messy hair and the cocky walk? He slouches a lot?"

"Arthur," she filled in.

"Arthur. You and him seem to have got *a lot* further than the school has, if I'm not mistaken."

Grace shrugged. She guessed that was true… The school hadn't really done anything, whereas they'd uncovered potential motives, clues and a whole bunch of secrets. OK, so they weren't the *right* secrets … but they'd still done some first-class journalistic snooping. They'd made a lot of mistakes, but maybe they *could* get somewhere with this after all.

"Thanks, Dad," Grace said.

"No problem. Now, eat your soup." Grace's dad stood up and crossed the room to the doorway. He winked at Grace one final time before shutting the door behind him.

A fresh glimmer of determination stirred in Grace. They'd come so far… Maybe they didn't have to give up on finding the thief just yet? She sat down to eat her soup and thought about all of the recordings she and *Radio Royalty* had done so far. There was something that still didn't quite add up.

The slime.

The glove had turned out to be nothing. A waste of time, a fool's errand, a red herring. But what about the slime? When they'd suspected Nikita and Misha, Grace had wondered if the slime was actually jelly. When Roddy and Bea were the prime suspects, she'd thought it might be hair gel. When Arthur and Kieran had been suspicious of Jordan, they wondered if it was glue from the set of the school play. But the more she thought about it, the more

Grace realized that nothing to do with the slime had been proven and nothing had been disproven.

That meant any one of their theories could still be possible. The answer was still out there *somewhere*.

But how would she find out which one was right?

As Grace finished her soup and went over every possible way forward, one thing became clear: she needed help.

It killed her a little bit inside... Although she desperately wanted a good friend, Grace took pride in being a lone wolf in her work. She was the girl in class who everyone asked for help – never the girl asking. But going solo hadn't worked out for anyone so far, had it? Originally, she'd thought herself infallible. She didn't think she could be wrong about anything. And look how that had turned out! She'd never imagined that she might learn something from someone else, but it seemed that she had.

There was only one person who could help her out of this mess. Putting her pride to one side and gritting her teeth, Grace started typing out a plea for help.

THE CASE MUST GO ON

[Cue backing track to Dancing Dad, album
track 4, intro 5 secs…]
MR MCLEAN: "Ooh, see that lad,
He's a dad,
Yeah he's the baddest dad…"
[Into verse 1. Into chorus.]

Arthur stared at his phone screen. When it had
first beeped, he'd had to blink a few times to
check his eyes weren't deceiving him. But no, it
really was a message from Bestie.

Need to talk to you in school tomorrow. Somewhere private. GB

Of course she signed off her messages "GB", he thought. That was so Grace. She'd probably manage to sound important and official if she wanted to borrow a stapler.

But in his heart Arthur knew it wasn't about that. He hoped he wasn't right, but he feared that Grace wanted to restart the investigation. Did the girl never know when to give up?!

"Who is it, Arthur?" His dad nudged him. "Girlfriend?"

He gave a cheesy wink to all the other "Lad Dadz". One of the Dadz wolf-whistled and another shouted, "Oi oi!"

Arthur cringed. He was about to answer a definitive *no*, when his mum, who was bringing in a tray of snacks, snorted.

"*Girlfriend*? I don't think so, dear," she said.

They both cackled.

Arthur had started the conversation feeling embarrassed and now he was offended too. Which was the worst combination, because he was too mortified to defend himself. But what was so funny about the idea of him having a girlfriend?

"What about Kieran?" his dad asked. "He's always been popular with the girls. I hear from his parents that he's quite mysterious these days. This time next year he'll probably be an official *moody teenager.*"

Mysterious?! Arthur grinned at the thought of his goofy, warm, open-hearted pal seeming mysterious.

"Yeah, give us the goss, Arthur," Arthur's mum chimed in. "Has Kieran got a girlfriend?"

Arthur shook his head non-committally. He *obviously* wasn't going to discuss this with his parents.

"Ah look, we're making him uncomfortable," said Arthur's mum. "It's OK, Arthur – you boys keep your secrets!"

Arthur sighed. It wasn't like he actually *had* any secrets. Not about girls anyway. But he was relieved to be free from questioning.

Arthur's dad picked up his guitar. "Right, Ladz. Let's take it from the top of *Smells Like Dad Bants*."

Clashing drums and thudding bass filled the garage once more, and Arthur watched as his mum bopped along. Despite all her "he'll never make it" and "he's wasting his time" speeches, he could tell she actually liked watching him. They'd first met at one of his dad's concerts, after all. Arthur would usually have blushed at the sound of his dad's cheesy songs and his mum's terrible dancing, but today he was just pleased to have been allowed out of his room.

His parents were still mad at him, obviously, but when Kirsty told them that he'd been sitting in his room pretending to record a show-and-tell with his odd sock collection they'd softened a bit. Since his dad's gig on Friday night had gone so well, the band had decided they wanted someone to record a *Lad Dadz: Journey to Fame* documentary and Arthur would be the perfect person to do it, since he was temporarily banned from recording for Listen Up. All the Ladz added an *o* on to the end of their names for the band – Stevo, Marco, Paulo, Haroldo – and his dad's bandmate Stevo had brought a dusty old mic with him. The documentary would be no *Radio Royalty*, and Stevo's mic was no Mikey, but Arthur was pleased to have any mic back in his hands and relieved that his parents were joking around with him again.

"This one's for my sauce pot!" Arthur's dad called out to Arthur's mum as he wiggled his hips. Arthur's mum giggled.

Arthur shut his eyes and held out the mic blindly. *Nothing to see, nothing to see, nothing to see,* he told himself.

As the rehearsal went on, Arthur tried to accept that for the time being this would be it for him. Making a documentary about Lad Dadz, doing his homework, maybe playing some football with Kieran. He tried not to think about the message from Grace, he really tried … but his phone was burning a hole in his pocket.

He didn't reply during rehearsal. He didn't reply as all the Lad Dadz packed up their gear, or even after they went home. He didn't reply as he helped his dad clean the house or while he watched a game show with his mum. It was safer just to leave it alone, wasn't it? The investigation was over. If anyone so much as caught a whiff of him or Grace with a microphone or going anywhere near a member of the chess crew they'd both be dead.

But … it was rude not to reply at all, right? Maybe it was nothing to do with the case at all. Maybe Grace needed something else. Maybe he'd dropped something in the hut and she'd picked it up and needed to return it to him.

That was what he told himself as he got ready for bed that night. That was what he told himself as he slipped Stevo's mic into his rucksack. That was what he told himself as he replied:

OK. Meet you at break in the old teachers' wing.

The next day Arthur couldn't concentrate on any of his lessons. He felt like he might throw up. Going down this path again felt like opening a can of worms. He was about to message Grace and tell her he changed his mind, when the most unlikely student cornered him in the corridor.

Jordan Baptiste.

He seemed to appear out of the shadows. How on earth did he manage to creep around so successfully, Arthur wondered? He rested a hand on Arthur's shoulder.

"Arthur, my friend," he said in a low tone.

"Um, hi, Jordan," Arthur replied.

"Forgive the interruption to your morning, but I had to address that which has been weighing on my shoulders."

"Er, sure? Look, Jordan, I'm sorry we accused…"

Jordan put a finger to his lips. "Please, say no more."

Arthur stopped.

"You were right, Arthur McLean. Perhaps I was not so impervious to fault as I cared to admit."

Impervious?

"But let me explain. I have known highs, I have known lows. I've been the winner and the loser. I've tasted glory and had it snatched from my grasp." He closed his eyes, clearly thinking of the science prize, and the trophy. "Like most, I've ridden the waves of joy and suffering. I've had good hair days and bad. No one is without their troubles, their pressures, their pain. But the one time I feel I can escape it all? When I'm *acting*."

Arthur opened his mouth, then closed it again. He wasn't sure what to say.

Jordan went on. "I imagine you feel the same way doing your radio show. To stop feeling like oneself and be immersed fully in something one loves is a blessing – a gift – and to have it threatened..." He paused. "When Mr Pathak said the drama club might have to close, all I can say is I felt I would do anything to hold on to it. It's possible I went too far."

Arthur nodded. He actually understood. If someone said Listen Up was shutting down, he couldn't bear to think how he'd feel.

"Anyway, now I'll be doing dance lessons with Alan, at his request," Jordan said.

Arthur couldn't help but laugh. That was his punishment? Dancing with Alan? "Mate, that's definitely worse than detention."

Jordan's eyes twinkled and Arthur thought he saw the hint of a smile. "You never know. I might discover a hidden talent. Anyway, I just wanted to clear the air. No hard feelings for exposing my crimes. As to the trophy? I'm afraid you'll have to keep searching."

He put his hand out. Arthur shook it.

"Thanks, Jordan, I…"

The bell rang and he looked aside for a moment. When he looked back Jordan was gone, as if he had disappeared in a puff of smoke. How did he do that?!

Arthur trudged to lessons, still thinking about Jordan. He was mysterious, sure, and he'd made mistakes, but he'd owned up to them. Arthur really did believe it wasn't him. But then … he didn't really believe it was any of them any more!

His encounter with Jordan meant he hadn't had time to cancel on Grace, or at least, he was telling himself that's why he hadn't cancelled. Although he was afraid of going back to the investigation, their bizarre chat had stirred something in him. Jordan's passion for drama, and everything he did in the name of continuing to do what he loved, reminded him exactly how he felt about *Radio Royalty*. Was he going to just let it all go now?

When the bell rang to signal the end of the morning lessons, he packed up his bag with a shaking hand. He hadn't even told Kieran about this shady meeting. When Kieran asked him where he was going at break time, he said he was going for some extra maths help. Which, he noticed with a pang, Kieran believed all too easily.

Kieran waved him off, but as soon as he turned a corner, Arthur bolted in the opposite direction. Even though it killed Arthur to lie to his best mate, he knew Kieran had well and truly given up on the investigation. Kieran's parents were even stricter than his were, and Arthur didn't want to feel responsible for dragging him into any more trouble. Plus, even if Kieran had wanted to come, if they all disappeared together it might raise suspicion. If people saw Kieran hanging around they'd assume

Arthur was close by, because they were usually inseparable. Arthur hated it, but Kieran going about his normal day gave Arthur good cover.

If anyone saw Grace and Arthur together, however... Well, no one would suspect them of working together anytime soon.

As Arthur crept along the dusty old hallways, it felt even spookier than last time they'd been here. For one, he'd had the others with him then, including Kieran pretending to be a ghostbuster. This time he was all alone.

Arthur tiptoed further along the windy halls, hoping Bestie had got the message and was already waiting for him in the abandoned classroom. What if she hadn't seen it? Now that he thought about it, she hadn't *actually* replied. What if he was totally alone in this dark, empty building? His footsteps echoed eerily around the empty space. Finally, he reached the right room.

"G ... Grace?" His voice broke as he called to her. "Are you here?"

There was no response. He looked into the darkness. It didn't seem like anyone was there. Arthur's heart started beating at double-speed.

Then a footstep sounded.

"Who ... who's there?" he stuttered.

What if Grace wasn't coming? What if the thief had been following him, seeking his or her revenge for all the trouble Arthur had caused them?

A disembodied face suddenly appeared in the darkness, a torch lighting it from underneath.

"BOO!" a voice called out.

Arthur shrieked and fell backwards over a table. Soft laughter echoed around the empty classroom.

Bestie.

"Who did you think it was?" Grace's laughs continued to bounce off the walls. "Oh, Arthur, you should have seen your face!"

Arthur pouted and stood up.

"That wasn't funny," he said, dusting himself down.

"What, you're the only one who can play pranks?"

Arthur didn't want to say it, but ... well, *yes*. Bestie was fun, but she was usually so focused that he hadn't expected it.

"Guess I've taken a leaf out of your book." Grace smiled.

Hang on ... did Grace Best just *sort of* give him a compliment? And was she seriously wasting time playing tricks on him instead of getting on with the matter at hand? Arthur thought he might fall backwards all over again, this time in shock. He had to admit it: her joke had been funny.

"So, let's get down to business then."

Ah, there was the Bestie Arthur knew.

"Yeah, well, *you* called this meeting," he replied. "So…?"

"So." Grace took a deep breath. "I don't think we should give up."

Arthur's heart stilled. He had known this was coming and yet he wasn't totally prepared for it.

"We?" he repeated.

Grace sighed and looked towards the ground.

"Well, working against each other didn't get us very far, did it?" she mumbled finally. "I figured out some stuff on my own, but … well, you and Kieran did too. Maybe if we stop fighting each other and combine our skills we might actually crack it."

Grace had said her whole little speech while staring at her shoes. Arthur could tell this was eating her up. The great Grace Best asking for help? She'd changed.

But then … so had Arthur. Once upon a time he would have lorded this moment over her. But after everything that had happened and all that it had cost them both, he just wanted to solve this case once and for all. He needed his radio show back, and finding the thief was key to that happening. They had to prove to their parents, and to Ms Lyall, that their investigations weren't just annoying mischief but true, groundbreaking journalism.

"I'm in," Arthur said firmly. He pulled Stevo's

mic out of his rucksack. "And I brought *this*."

Grace saw the microphone and her face broke into a wide grin. "I'm not even going to ask," she said. She reached her hand out to Arthur.

"To working together?"

Arthur reached out and shook it. "To working together. Now, what have you got?"

AN UNLIKELY ALLY

[Cue dramatic music.]

ARTHUR: "There is a world that has been out of reach, until now… Two offices lie side by side, but could not be more different. One — belonging to the commonly sighted Mr Pathak — has students in and out all day, and the other… Well, no student has crossed its boundaries in years. Here, we approach the natural habitat of the elusive Ms Grant. Often in hiding, sightings of this enigmatic teacher are rare."

Grace *must* have had a breakthrough, Arthur thought, otherwise she wouldn't have brought him here. As he suspected, she had reached into her pocket and pulled out a whole new lead.

"OK, so it's not exactly fresh evidence," Grace admitted sheepishly. "I've actually had this the whole time. But—"

"You've had this the whole time and you kept it to yourself?!" Arthur gestured wildly.

"You don't even know what it is yet," said Grace.

"Well… I'm still indignant."

"We only started working together five minutes ago, remember?" Grace pointed out.

Arthur stuck out his bottom lip in acceptance. If he'd found a clue last week he probably wouldn't have told her about it either. "Fine. Go on."

"So you remember how, the day after the theft, Ms Lyall let me borrow the glove?"

Arthur nodded.

"And she told me about the slime?"

Arthur nodded.

"Well, I asked her what they were going to do about the slime. And she said, 'Clean it up.' So *I* said that was a waste of good evidence. And *she* said, 'Leaving it there is a health and safety hazard so stop interfering.'"

Arthur smiled. Grace even bossed Ms Lyall around. He had to admire her for that.

"So, before she sent Alan in with his … mop…"

They both paused and stifled their laughter.

"Before Alan cleaned it up," Grace continued, "I went in and took a bit. Not loads, because then they'd have noticed. But I got a decent sample."

She finally held up the thing she'd taken out of her pocket. It was a clear plastic bag with a trace of greyish-greenish slime inside. As she held it up she wrinkled her nose.

"It's a bit gross."

"You can say that again," said Arthur, tilting his head sideways and frowning at the sludgey mess. "It's cool, but … how is this going to help us?"

"Well, so far we have three different theories about what it is," Grace said.

Arthur nodded and counted them off on his fingers.

"1) Nikita or Misha's jelly,

2) Roddy's hair gel,

3) Jordan's glue."

"If we analyse it we could *surely* find out what it is and which of the theories fits. The only problem is…"

"We don't have a lab? And we're not scientists? And we basically have no idea what we're doing?" Arthur suggested.

"Um, yes." Grace shrugged.

They both fell silent, thinking long and hard. Arthur raised a hand to his jaw and stroked an imaginary beard. There were labs at school but breaking into school property hadn't gone so well for them the first time. And once they did get in what would they do? Neither of them had the first clue about science! Arthur supposed they could ask someone sciencey… He was sure there were loads of kids who would help them. But asking other kids to get involved was a risk factor. What if the kid got in trouble because of them, or what if someone told?

"We could ask someone who does science. But we can't break into the labs," Grace said, voicing his thoughts. "We can't risk getting caught again."

Come on, Arthur, he thought to himself. *Where's your creative brainwave?* If ever he needed one to hit, surely it was now…

And then it did.

His face lit up. "Grace, what if we weren't breaking in?" He took hold of her shoulders.

"What if we had a teacher's permission?"

For a moment Grace looked at him like he had a chicken sitting on his head. Then she caught on to his meaning. She locked eyes with his. And breathed in sharply.

"Do you think it would work?"

"We won't know until we try." Arthur released her from his grip.

Grace beamed. "I think it just might be crazy enough. Arthur, you genius!" She leapt up in the air. Grace's unexpected praise took them both by surprise and Arthur raised his eyebrows in surprise.

"Um, let's go," she coughed.

With that, they headed off to chase their one, final lead. Their one, final chance.

When they first knocked on the door no one answered.

"Well, that's anti-climatic," said Arthur.

"Do you think she's out?"

Grace shook her head. "She's *never* out. She pretends to be so everyone will leave her alone. But I bet she's in there doing some sort of experiment. If we wait here long enough she'll think we've gone."

Arthur put his finger to his lips and they both waited. Minutes passed and, sure enough, they heard a quiet *bang!* from inside, followed by a "Huzzah!"

Arthur was so glad he was working with Grace now. She noticed important details that would have slipped by him and Kieran. He knocked again.

"Oh *all right*, I'm just coming," said a voice.

There was the sound of a chair wheeling towards them and then the door slowly opened, revealing a wisp of grey hair, colourful glittering earrings and bright purple eye shadow.

Ms Grant: the science teacher.

"What is it?" she barked.

"Good afternoon, Ms G. Me and Grace here were wondering if we could come in and ask you a few questions?"

He held out Stevo's mic and prayed word hadn't spread to Ms Grant that they were currently banned from doing their radio shows. The plan was to get Ms Grant chatting about the science prize, which she judged every year, and then asking for help with their "failed entry" to see where they went wrong, except, obviously, there was no entry to speak of and there were *so* many ways their plan could go awry. Ms Grant might not let them in at all, she might know that they'd never entered the science prize, and even if she thought they *had* entered it, she might not agree to help them.

She tucked a strand of hair behind her ear, making one of her giant earrings wobble. "No time."

"Oh, yes, we understand you're super busy," Arthur said. "What are you up to?"

Ms Grant's eyes shifted to one side. "...Marking."

Marking, thought Grace. *Sure.* Like *that* would explain all the explosion sounds they'd heard.

"*Of course* you are," said Arthur. "Even so, we wondered if we might tempt you for just two minutes? We had a few quick questions about this year's very exciting science prize!" He flashed her a huge grin.

"Oh, all right then," Ms Grant said begrudgingly. "Two minutes."

Grace was so glad she was working with Arthur now. He really knew how to get people talking.

They followed Ms Grant into her lair. If

Alan's hut had been something to behold, it was nothing compared to this. Ms Grant had rolled down the blinds, but brought in extra lamps so the room was incredibly bright. The walls were lined with rows upon rows of strange objects in jars. Among them Grace spotted what looked like a pickled kiwi-fruit and a shoe. On the table some dark purple liquid bubbled away in a jar.

"What's that?" asked Arthur.

"…Ribena."

"Of course it is."

Arthur continued to ask Ms Grant about various strange items around the room, and received similarly short and cagey answers. Eventually he clapped his hands together. "So, Ms Grant, the prize is in its fifth year now and growing year by year. Grace here actually entered and was thoroughly disappointed not to win, weren't you, Grace?"

"Err, yes?" said Grace. Ugh, she *hated* lying.

But she was only lying in an attempt to find out the truth, she told herself.

They waited for Ms Grant to call them out, but her face remained expressionless. It seemed she *didn't* know whether or not Grace had entered. *Phew.* Their plan was actually working so far – they were inside Ms Grant's office and she was actually talking! Sort of.

"I think this was the science prize's biggest year yet," Arthur continued. "How many entrants *did* you receive, exactly?"

"Oh, about eighty," said Ms Grant. She reached for a file in the bottom drawer of her desk and began flipping through the papers inside it. Grace peered over her shoulder and caught a few familiar names: Nikita Klimach, Misha Klimach, Jordan Baptiste. Ms Grant carried on counting. Grace widened her eyes at Arthur. If Ms G flipped through them all she'd see that Grace wasn't there.

Arthur put his hand on the papers to stop her flicking through them. "No need to count exactly, Ms G!" About eighty, gosh! That's impressive. And you started the science prize five years ago, didn't you? How many entries did you receive in your *first* year?"

Ms Grant eyed Arthur's hand. He removed it quickly. She put the papers back in the folder and Grace breathed a sigh of relief. "Nine," Ms Grant answered.

"Wow!" Grace leaned over to Stevo's mic. "So over eight times as many in five years. That's amazing."

"Yes," said Ms Grant.

Grace was glad this wasn't a real interview. She'd got more enthusiasm out of the objects in her bedroom than Ms Grant.

"What kind of stuff did you get?" Arthur went on.

"Oh, all sorts. Nikita's winning glitter volcano

of course. Another student attempted a fizzing slime volcano which was brave...There was glowing water, balloon speakers..."

"Amazing. Look, we know you're busy so we'll get right down to it," Arthur continued. "Grace here was hoping for some hints and tips to give her more of a chance for next year."

"Yes," Grace said. "I tried to make, er, frozen slime and, er, it didn't freeze." She pulled the slime out of her bag and passed it to Ms Grant. "I wondered if we could, er, analyse the slime to see where I went wrong?"

She grimaced. She was a *terrible* liar. Arthur raised his eyes to the ceiling. This was the final stage of the plan and it *needed* to work.

For a while Ms Grant said nothing. She turned the plastic bag over in her hands. And then:

"My social skills may be somewhat sub-par compared to my scientific ones, but you do not want my help with frozen slime. You did *not* enter the science prize, Ms Best. Nor have you ever shown much interest in my class, although you do well enough. If you wanted to make frozen slime I have no doubt you'd be entirely capable of the task."

Grace's heart sank.

"I also happen to know that you two are currently banned from recording any radio shows. You aren't friends. In fact, this is the first time I've seen you in the same room without bickering. So tell me, why are you *really* here?"

Grace felt like she wanted to cry. They hadn't fooled anybody – Ms Grant was well and truly on to them. Their last chance had been blown and Ms Grant was going to call Ms Lyall and dob them in. After all the trouble she'd got into, Grace couldn't imagine what her parents were going to say now. She looked across at Arthur, who had paled. The same thoughts were obviously going through his mind. Forget being banned from recording for Listen Up for a week or two… What if they were banned for ever?

"Ms Grant—" Arthur's voice was cracking. He looked like he might be sick.

"No lies. Why do you want my help analysing this piece of gunk?" She peered at the green slime zipped up in the plastic bag.

Arthur and Grace looked at each other. Grace waited for Arthur to say something charming and clever and get them out of this mess, but she knew the truth: nothing anyone said would get them out of *this*. There was no other option… Grace knew they had to come clean.

"We're still looking for the Victory Road thief, Ms Grant," she said. Arthur looked at her like she'd gone crazy. He started miming moving his hand across his neck to get her to stop, but Grace ignored him. She told Ms Grant all about the glove, the slime and about the interviews they'd done – how it had led them to nothing except trouble. In all the movies, it was coming clean and laying all their cards and emotions out on the table that helped the heroes get what they needed, right?!

The whole time Grace was talking, Ms Grant stared at her without the flicker of a reaction. Grace hoped beyond hope that underneath her blank expression her heart was melting.

"So you see, Ms Grant," Grace concluded, "this bit of gunk is our last hope. We really need you to help us analyse it, or we'll never find the Victory Road thief. Everything we've been through will have been for *nothing*."

Ms Grant took a long breath and peered at the slime once more. Grace's hands were in fists. Her neck had practically disappeared into her shoulders she was so tense. She was sure this heartfelt plea couldn't have fallen on deaf ears. It *had* to have worked.

"I'm sorry, but I don't care about the Victory

Road thief," Ms Grant said at last. "Good day, Mr McLean, Miss Best."

Grace couldn't believe it. How could *anyone* have heard their story and be so unmoved?

"But, Ms G…" Arthur started.

"It's probably time to leave now. Unless you want me to tell Ms Lyall about your little visit?" Ms Grant raised an eyebrow.

Arthur nodded and started heading towards the door. But Grace had picked up on something she said. Ms Grant didn't care about them, or their radio shows. She didn't care about the thief. But she *did* care about one thing.

"That's such a shame," said Grace, her voice shaking. This was a risky move. Ms Grant hadn't handed them over to Ms Lyall yet, but they were on thin ice. "I guess we'll have to find out what this gross goop is made out of by ourselves then."

Arthur stopped at the door and turned back. Ms Grant pursed her lips and began playing with her dangly earring. It was the biggest rise they'd managed to get out of her so far.

"Catching thieves through forensics... It's not about crime, really, is it, Arthur?" Grace winked. "It's about *science*."

Ms Grant narrowed her eyes at Grace. After a moment's silence, she undid the brake on her wheelchair and rolled towards Arthur, who was still standing by the door.

"Congratulations, Miss Best, you've captured my attention," she said.

Arthur and Grace gawked at each other. They could hardly believe it! Was she really going to help them?

"Come on!" Ms Grant called. She'd already wheeled halfway down the corridor, back towards the science labs. "Do you want my help or not?"

Grace and Arthur fist-bumped and began sprinting after her.

THE RESULTS ARE IN

[Intro: *Radio Royalty* jingle. Cue bubbling lab sound effects.]

ARTHUR: "So, to break this down: two parts glue, one part water, one part sodium … tetris … er, what was that thing you said again?"

MS GRANT: "Sodium tetraborate."

ARTHUR: "Right, combined and stirred slowly… The result? Well, scientific expert Ms Grant is with us now to talk us through her microscopic analysis of slime…"

When they reached the science labs, Ms Grant

reached inside her pocket for her set of keys. As she unlocked the door, Arthur and Grace stood nervously beside her, shifting from side to side.

It opened. They were in. They were really in! They were *finally* going to catch the thief, get the scoop of a lifetime and prove themselves to their parents and Ms Lyall!

"Jackets off. Lab coats on. Sanitizer, gloves and goggles are in the corner." But you could tell she was excited at the prospect of tracking down a thief using science.

Grace and Arthur followed her instructions. Arthur drew a pair of eyes on his goggles and when he put them on he looked like an alien. Grace giggled.

"No time for that, Mr McLean." Ms Grant put on her own lab coat and gloves and gestured for Grace to hand her the sample. Out of a drawer she pulled a swab, a pipette and what looked like two pieces of clear plastic.

"Hold this." Ms Grant gestured for Grace to hold the plastic and the pipette. She unfastened the bag of slime and reached the swab into it, smearing it in the greeny, greyish goo.

"Separate the two pieces of plastic and hand me one," she instructed Grace, who did as she was told. Grace smirked. She could tell Arthur wanted a task too, but he was clearly being left out because of his alien goggles.

Ms Grant took the first piece of plastic from Grace's gloved hand. "Really quite disgusting," she remarked as she rubbed the swab of slime on it. "Now, Miss Best, pop the pipette in this."

Grace stuck the pipette in a beaker of water as Ms Grant held out the first piece of plastic covered in slime. "Now put one drop on the specimen. Careful to only add one drop, no more."

Arthur blew a raspberry in frustration. Grace was getting to do all the good stuff! He watched her lean in and with a steady hand carefully place a single drop on to the plastic.

"Very good, Miss Best," Ms Grant complimented. "It's a shame you're more interested in your radio show than science. You could be magnificent."

Grace smiled and could have sworn that Ms Grant almost showed expression on her face as she looked back at her. Arthur coughed as a reminder that, yes, he was still standing there, but no more praise was forthcoming.

"I'm going to cover what we're doing," suggested Arthur. "We might need to listen back later. Plus, once we find the culprit everyone will want to know how, and we'll have this audio!"

Grace agreed and Arthur began recording.

"Now, I'll hold the bottom while you very carefully place the second piece of plastic on top," Ms Grant explained. "Be careful to position it right first time, as you don't want to damage or lose the sample."

Very, very slowly, Grace put the slide together.

"Perfect," said Ms Grant. "Now we have our slide ready for the microscope."

"So what is it exactly that we're doing, Miss G?" asked Arthur.

"This is called microscopic analysis. We might be able to tell what the components of the slime are by looking at them on a microscopic level."

"And … in English?" asked Arthur.

"We might be able to tell what the slime is made of by looking at it very, very closely using this excellent machine here."

"Cool, thanks."

Ms Grant's giant earrings quivered as she hovered over the microscope. Arthur peered over Ms Grant's shoulder.

"Space, Mr McLean," Ms Grant said.

Arthur nodded and stepped back.

"And what if we can't tell from using the

microscope?" Grace asked.

"Then we'd have to resort to confirmatory testing involving separation and identification of the separate components of the substance. Methods include gas chromatography, capillary electrophoresis and wet chemistry."

Grace and Arthur looked at each other. Arthur didn't even bother asking her what that meant in English. It sounded *complicated* and definitely not like something that could be done over their lunch break. Grace prayed the microscopic analysis worked.

It seemed to take *for ever*. Ms Grant kept making noises like "Hmm," and "Oh," and "Ah." Grace couldn't stand the tension. She and Arthur were both bouncing on their toes. Were they going to find the thief or not?! The whole investigation had basically come down to this moment!

"Anything, Miss G?" Grace could hear the desperation in Arthur's voice.

Ms Grant sat up from the microscope. "What did you say the options were?" she asked.

"Jelly, hair gel or glue," repeated Grace.

Nikita and Misha, Bea and Roddy or Jordan. Who was it going to be?

"It's definitely not glue," said Ms Grant. "The components are all wrong. Glue looks very distinctive under a microscope."

Even though her and Arthur were working together now, Grace couldn't help but feel a *little* smug that Jordan, Arthur's prime suspect, seemed to have been ruled out. Arthur's shoulders slumped.

Ms Grant peered back through the viewer. "It doesn't look like hair gel either," she said.

So not Roddy and Bea. Grace couldn't help but be a little disappointed. Still, if it wasn't Jordan and it wasn't Roddy and Bea, that only left one pair of thieves. Nikita and Misha!

Grace started jumping up and down and

Arthur raised his hands in the air. "Grace, we've got it!" he shouted. "It's jelly! It was definitely…"

"Don't get too excited," said Ms Grant. "The cells don't look like jelly either, I'm afraid. Not like any jelly I've seen. So … I'm not sure."

Grace landed back on the ground with a thud. Arthur brought his arms down.

A lump rose in Grace's throat. "What do you mean?"

"Come and look." Ms Grant beckoned them over. "See the shape of the cells. They're not big and block-ish, like jelly."

Grace peered through the viewer and looked at the substance. The lump in her throat got bigger. Ms Grant was right; the cells didn't look like large or square at all. She felt like an Olympian who'd just fallen at the final hurdle. How could they still have no conclusive evidence? What was this goo and how did it get on the stage?

She sagged down on a chair as Arthur moved forwards to look through the microscope. They were never going to figure it out. It was over. Grace was ready to pack up. She started taking off her gloves.

"Come on, Arthur, let's go. Thanks for all your—"

"What could it be, Ms G? Any ideas?" Arthur interrupted as he peered down at the sample, unwilling to let go.

Ms Grant put her hand on her chin. "If I'm not mistaken, from the bubbles and the strange colour, I'd say it looks like some sort of horrible, acidic drink you kids love so much. But it's too thick," she puzzled. "Strange."

Grace sat bolt upright in her chair. She was so glad Arthur had given her that one last push, just as she was ready to give up.

"Ms G, didn't you say you received a fizzing slime volcano entry for the science prize this year? Could this substance be not a fizzy drink, but fizzy *slime*?"

Arthur looked up from the microscope. They both stared at Ms Grant.

Ms Grant tucked a stray hair behind her glasses. "Well, I suppose it *could*…"

"Who entered it, Ms G? Who was it?" Grace pressed.

"I'm afraid I can't tell you that. Anyway, the science prize was months ago! And why would someone be carrying it in their bag? I doubt that has anything to do with your investigation, Ms Best."

"Did the entry work?" Grace went on frantically. "Did the fizzing slime volcano work?"

Ms Grant thought back. "No," she answered after a second. "No, it wasn't quite as successful as Nikita's volcano, I'm afraid. The eruption was slow and unimpressive."

"ARTHUR," Grace almost shouted.

"What? What is it?"

"I think, I don't know but, I'm not sure…" Grace babbled.

"Grace, *what is it?*" Arthur came close to her. Grace was ripping off her gloves and her lab coat.

"I think I might have remembered something. I think… I think I know who it was. Come on!" Grace raced to the edge of the classroom and hung her coat on the peg. Arthur followed her.

"Come on, Arthur!" She beckoned him frantically.

"Thank you SO MUCH, Ms Grant, you've been amazingly incredibly super helpful. To us and to science!" she yelled. Ms Grant nodded at her with a small smile and raised her goggles in a salute.

But Grace and Arthur were already speeding down the corridor.

AN UNEXPECTED RIVALRY

[Cue cheering crowd sound effects.]
ARTHUR: "Grace picks up speed as she gets a clear run of the corridor, after she expertly dodges a stray first year…"
GRACE: "Oooh, but McLean's progress slows as he fails to notice an unexpected pen and goes skidding to the left…"

"Grace, seriously though," Arthur wheezed from just behind her. "Where are we … going?!"

"I know who it was! I'm positive! We've got to get to Classroom 2B!" Grace called out.

"Are you sure?" Arthur yelled. "Because we've been here before. Are we really just going to make quick accusations all over again? Each time we looked like right *doughnuts*, as Kieran would say."

She stopped suddenly in the corridor and Arthur collided into her back. Some students in the corridor mockingly rolled their eyes at them as they passed. Grace and Arthur squabbling was a common sight. If only they knew they were actually working together for once.

"You're right," said Grace. "Help me?"

Before Arthur could comment on the great Bestie actually asking for help, Grace took her phone out of her pocket, going straight to *Radio Royalty's* past episodes.

"Look, Grace, I know you're mine and Kieran's number one fan, and I'm flattered, but now's not really the time," he joked.

"Ha-ha," Grace mocked.

She opened up the interview with Misha, skipped to about seven minutes in and hit play.

"Do *you* know the secret to her winning volcano?" said Arthur's voice.

"I know to make a volcano you add vinegar to baking powder. That's about it. As I said, Nikita's the scientist," said Misha's voice.

Grace hit pause. "Now's where I need you," she said. "Do you still have your interview with Nikita? The one you couldn't use?"

Arthur frowned at her. "Um, yeah, I think so." He pulled out his phone and flipped through old saved clips. When he found the right one he handed his phone to Grace.

She took it to about five minutes in and hit play.

"So how did you make your volcano, anyway?" An exasperated Kieran sounded from the phone. Arthur cringed, remembering how terrible the interview was.

"Well, everyone knows the basics are vinegar and baking soda. But that's all I can divulge, I'm afraid," said Nikita.

Grace smiled. She hit play on both clips in turn.

"Baking soda."

"Baking powder."

"Baking soda."

"Baking powder."

Grace smiled wider. "AHA!" she cried.

Arthur blinked. "What's the difference? Aren't they the same?"

"No!" Grace could barely contain herself. "Classic mistake. They *look* the same, but they are different! One time I…" Grace tailed off.

"One time…?" Arthur went on.

Grace sighed. She'd started now and she *hated* being that person who'd start a sentence and refuse to finish it. "I was helping my mum bake some chin chin," she mumbled. "I used baking soda instead of baking powder and it went *totally* wrong. They tasted all metallic and weird. Lucas and Nathan spat them out and pelted them at each other... It was a total disaster." Grace shuddered.

"What's chin chin again?" asked Arthur.

"It's a Nigerian snack," Grace muttered.

She winced, waiting for the inevitable weird look. But it didn't come. "Cool." Arthur shrugged.

Grace felt herself relax. She carried on. "Anyway, I know for a *fact* if you use one instead of the other in baking, you might not get the same result," Grace explained. "I *bet* it's the same in science!" She pulled up the recording again and took it back to just before seven minutes. She hit play.

"Did you enter the science prize?" It was Arthur's voice.

"No, Nikita's the scientist," said Misha's voice.

Grace paused. Arthur's eyes lit up. She played the clip again.

"Did you enter the science prize?"

"No, Nikita's the scientist."

"*No way,*" he whispered. Back in Ms Grant's office, when she was flicking through the science prize entries, they'd both seen the same name pop up.

Misha Klimach.

"She lied about entering the science prize…" breathed Arthur.

Grace beamed. "All this time we thought Nikita and Misha would be working together. We assumed Jordan was the one who was jealous of Nikita's science prize win. But what if…"

"What if it was her *sister*?" said a voice from the doorway beside them.

Arthur and Grace both spun round and peered at the figure emerging from classroom 2B.

Misha was coming towards them.

She seemed to tower over Grace and Arthur, even though she was quite short. She was scowling. They inhaled deeply and Arthur switched on the mic as they faced her. They tried to stand bravely, but both their legs were trembling. They were having a live confrontation with the *actual Victory Road thief!*

"So, you found me. OK, I give up, you found me. Tell the world!" She gestured to the mic. "Tell the world I stole it! I stole the trophy! The slime on the floor was mine! It dripped off my bag, OK!"

Grace couldn't believe this was actually happening. Misha was confessing … and they were *recording* it. In her wildest dreams she couldn't have imagined a better moment.

"Wait, I'm still seriously confused," said Arthur. "How did slime, from a science prize that was months ago, get on the floor at the chess tournament?"

Misha's face crumpled.

"Because it went wrong, didn't it, Misha," Grace filled in. "And you've been trying to get it right ever since."

Misha put her head in her hands. "So many times!" she cried. "So many times I've tried to get that stupid volcano to work properly! On the morning of the chess tournament one of the volcanoes had such a delayed reaction it exploded all over me just as I was about to leave for school. I thought I'd got it all, but it must have been dripping off my clothes. Why, *why* does it never erupt like Nikita's does!" She raised her fists to the ceiling.

"Ah, I think we might be able to help you…" interjected Arthur. "So, we worked out it's the…"

"Not the time," Grace coughed under her breath. Arthur stopped talking.

"But *how*?" Grace went on. "How did you pick it up? What about your nickel allergy?"

"I used my shoes," Misha admitted. "I wore them on my hands. They're pumps so it worked. It wasn't the easiest to carry, but I managed it fast enough to slip it in my rucksack."

Her *shoes*?! Arthur and Grace felt like smacking their palms on their foreheads. Of course! Now it made sense why her footsteps were basically silent!

"But … *why*?" asked Arthur.

"Why?" Misha planted her hands on her hips.

"*Why*? How do you think it feels only winning competitions because of your sister? Never succeeding by yourself? No one believing in your abilities? No one noticing you unless you're by her side, being her *stooge*?" As Misha spoke she put air quotation marks around the word "stooge" with her hands. Arthur and Grace glanced at each other. That *was* the name they'd given the episode of Misha's interview…

"But you're a team!" Arthur shrugged.

"Yes, a team." Misha sighed. "And Nikita's always the star. Just *once* I wanted to win something for myself. To be my own person. You should hear our parents sometimes. It's all Nikita this and Nikita that… I thought that if I won the science prize…" She looked down at the floor. "I thought they might notice me too. But then who wins it? Nikita. Of course. When the chess tournament came along, I thought, *finally*! A chance to play as an individual instead of a pair! I trained so hard for that trophy. I neglected my chores, my homework, my *friends*... My parents were in the audience. I wanted them to finally see me for once! But I hadn't anticipated Jordan."

She sighed.

"He wanted it even more than I did. And who ended up in the final competing with him, once again?"

Arthur and Grace looked at each other. They could both empathize. Sometimes it felt like Arthur's sister Kirsty could do no wrong in his parents' eyes. And sometimes Grace's brothers' closeness made her feel like the odd one out.

"I bet your parents *do* notice you," said Arthur. "Nikita's just older, so sometimes it might feel like she does everything first. And better. I get it. I feel the same sometimes. But you can't go around stealing trophies..."

"I know, OK!" Misha cried. She looked like

she was on the verge of tears. "I know! And I didn't plan this! I wanted to be a winner, not a thief! But … when the lights went out … I saw a chance and I took it." She tugged a strand of dark hair behind her ear. Her usually intense eyes softened. "As soon as I did it I knew I'd made a terrible mistake. I spent the next two days trying to work out a way to get it back into Ms Lyall's office. But then…"

"Then…?" Arthur encouraged her.

Misha's eyes took on a distant, faraway look. She seemed as though she was lost in a terrible nightmare. "Then it disappeared."

Arthur and Grace blinked.

"What?" Grace's eyes darted back and forth, as if trying to work out the most difficult kind of long division. "What do you mean?"

"I was keeping it in my locker," Misha went on. "One day I went back there and found it gone, with a note in its place."

Arthur lowered the mic. Grace's eyebrows knitted together. What was she telling them?

"Let me get this straight," Arthur said. "You're saying that you stole the trophy and then someone *else* stole the trophy from *you*?"

"I know it sounds ridiculous!" Misha threw her hands up again. "But let me show you."

Arthur and Grace looked at each other. Arthur nodded.

"OK," Grace said finally. "Show us."

"But this better not be a wind-up!" Arthur warned.

"It's not, I swear it!" Misha wailed. "Come on, my locker's over here."

Grace shrugged at Arthur. They'd come so close…

Could there really be a *second* thief at large?!

STRIKING THE RIGHT NOTE

[Intro: *Best of the Best* jingle (7 secs). Cue presenter.]

GRACE: "Welcome, Misha, to *Inside Your Locker*. Please talk us through what all these treasures mean to you…"

MISHA: "Well, this is my pencil case, which my parents bought me when I first started at Victory Road…"

GRACE: "Such memories. And what about behind the big binder?"

MISHA: "My special lunchbox, which I've had with me since primary school…"

Arthur shook his head. Grace massaged her

temples. They'd well and truly riffled through the inside Misha's locker, which, it seemed, really did only contain a few books and notepads and a pencil case.

"See!" Misha peered inside. "There's nothing else in here! It's gone!"

Arthur sighed. How could they have come *this far* only to be thwarted *again*? "Show us the note," he ordered.

Misha unzipped her pencil case and unfolded a crumpled piece of paper. The three of them peered down at it. A short message had been scrawled in messy handwriting, using what looked like a blue fountain pen.

After all the trouble this trophy has caused, it's going to a better home.

"Arghhh!"
"Is this for real, Misha, or is it another game?"

Arthur's eyes locked on Misha's – he wasn't convinced yet. After all, how could they trust her word after she stole the trophy and lied about it?

"I swear," Misha promised. "I wanted to give it back. I realized what a fool I'd been. I acted in the heat of the moment, but…" She sniffed. "I love my sister. I want her to do well. And I don't want to win by stealing."

Grace leaned her head against the lockers. Arthur kept looking Misha dead in the eye. He liked to rely on his gut and although he hadn't been a hundred per cent accurate throughout this investigation, he had at least sensed when something was off. Misha really did feel sorry for what she'd done.

"We've got nothing, Arthur," Grace mumbled into the wall. "Nothing! Again!"

Arthur grimaced. Grace was right. "Can I see that, Misha?" He gestured to the note.

Misha nodded and passed it over. "Keep it, please. I don't want to think about it any more."

"All right, thanks…" He folded up the note again and tucked it inside her jacket. "I guess we should go. Come on, Grace."

Grace seemed even more down about this being a dead end than any of the other leads so far. Arthur peeled her hands from the wall and led her back down the hallway. For once, they walked in silence. They'd finally got it right, and yet it was all still wrong. They couldn't air *this*. What an unsatisfying ending for their listeners. What an unsatisfying ending for them! This investigation had been the craziest of rollercoasters and had once again resulted in a missing trophy. They were both exhausted.

"I give up," Grace said, as they reached their afternoon lessons.

"Yup," Arthur agreed. "It's over. It's actually over."

And with heavy hearts they took their seats for English. The note from the real thief burned a hole in his pocket, but what good was it?

When the bell rang, Arthur caught up with Grace as they headed home for the day.

"Crazy day, huh?" he commented, more to himself than to her.

Grace nodded. They walked in silence for a few moments, contemplating their lunchtime events.

"Wanttodosomethingafterschool?" Arthur blurted.

Grace was so surprised she stopped walking. Had someone just invited her to hang out? Nothing to do with the radio? Just to spend time together? And Arthur McLean, no less?! This day really *wasn't* going the way she expected. But she couldn't help a warm feeling bubbling up in her stomach and spreading out through her limbs.

"Er, sure," she answered awkwardly.

"Um, OK," Arthur replied, equally awkwardly. He looked just as surprised by the invitation as she was, and now she'd said yes he seemed to hardly know what to do with himself. He'd forgotten how to walk properly and kept tripping over his feet, and he was staring at his hands like he'd never seen them before. Grace smiled. She didn't think she'd ever seen Arthur looking uncomfortable. It was nice to know that even the most confident boy in school felt embarrassed now and again.

Then a burst of panic shot through her.

"Err," she said suddenly. "As long as we go to your house? We can't go to mine." It was Nigerian Night and she didn't think she could bear it if Arthur didn't want to eat whatever her mum was making. That had happened with a friend from her primary school – she hadn't wanted to touch her okra soup so they had

to order her a pizza instead – and Grace still burned with humiliation when she thought about it. She hadn't invited anyone home for Nigerian Night since.

"Um, sure." Arthur looked confused, but he seemed to accept it. Grace breathed a sigh of relief.

As they approached the school gates Grace saw Kieran up ahead, waiting for Arthur. She felt a pang of jealousy until she remembered that Arthur had waited for *her* outside class.

Someone had waited for her! Even though she was still down about the investigation, an incredible feeling of lightness lifted her up. She actually felt like she understood the meaning of "a spring in one's step".

As Arthur and Grace walked towards him, Kieran looked between them like he was trying to figure something out. He waved cautiously like he might be the victim of a practical joke.

"Hey?" he said, the inflection in his voice rising like it was a question. "Are you coming to Arthur's, Grace?"

"Err, if that's OK." Suddenly Grace felt nervous. What if Kieran didn't want her there? What if she was stepping on his toes? But his face broke into a wide grin and she felt instantly at ease.

"Awesome," he said. "Let's ask Mrs McL if we can order pizzas. I'm getting pepperoni. Or maybe a meat supreme. Or should I get a ham and pineapple…?"

"He does this every time," Arthur fake whispered to Grace. "He'll *never* order a ham and pineapple but he always pretends to consider it."

Grace smiled. She didn't know Kieran that well but she did know that he really cared about food. As the three of them walked back to Arthur's, Kieran continued to list every possible kind of pizza he *might* order. Grace was still bummed about the still-missing trophy, but she couldn't remember the last time she'd felt so carefree or talked such rubbish.

When they got back to Arthur's they filled Kieran in on everything that had happened that day. Kieran couldn't believe it. He made them go through it all again, repeating every little detail. He listened to the recordings of Misha's confession, being careful to keep the volume down in case Arthur's parents heard. After all, they were all still officially banned from recording anything for Listen Up.

When he'd listened he sat back with his hands behind his head. "Woah," he said. "That's like … *woah*."

Arthur and Grace nodded. The disappointment in the air was tangible. Going through it all again with Kieran was like reliving it. They'd come *so close* to finding the trophy…

"So we have no idea where it is now?" Kieran asked. "Misha had no clues?"

"Only this note," said Arthur, pulling it out of his pocket and laying it on the table.

Kieran bent over it. "*After all the trouble this trophy has caused, it's going to a better home…*" he read to himself. "*After all the trouble this trophy has caused, it's going to a better home…* Nope. No idea. That could be literally anyone."

"We're right back at square one," Arthur agreed.

Kieran picked up the note to take a closer look. "Hey, what's this on the back?" he asked, turning it over.

All three of them leaned over it to get a better look. The back of the paper was lined, with black dots on.

"It's the back of a musical sheet," Arthur answered.

Just as he said this, the sound of 'Smells Like Dad Bants' filled the hallway. Arthur groaned. *Why?* Why on the night he brought Grace home for the first time? Couldn't *Lad Dadz* have picked another night to rehearse?

"Is that your dad?" Grace held her hand to her ear. The corner of her mouth crinkled in a smile.

"Yes," Arthur mumbled.

"I saw his flyer on Ms Lyall's desk after you had your meeting…" she continued.

"Look, don't, all right," said Arthur. "It's seriously embarrassing, I know."

"I wasn't going to say that, I…" Grace started, but Arthur had already got up and moved away from the sofa. His face had turned bright red. Carrying the note away with him, he sat down at the piano stool on the other side of the room.

Kieran pulled a "yikes" face at Grace. "Lad Dadz is a bit of a touchy subject," he whispered.

Grace couldn't imagine why Arthur was embarrassed, but knowing how she felt about her own family embarrassments, she didn't press it further.

On the other side of the room, Arthur prayed Grace wouldn't ask any more questions about the Ladz. Anyway, he'd become intrigued by the piece of music on the back of the note. Setting it down at the piano, he began to play the tune. It was a tiny piece of paper so there were only four notes on it.

"Where did you learn to—" Grace started to ask, but Kieran pulled his "yikes" grimace even wider.

Arthur kept playing, grateful for Kieran's interruption. He didn't want to have to answer that his musician dad taught him, because that would bring the conversation right back around to Lad Dadz.

For a moment, they all just listened to Arthur playing. As he played the notes over and over, a feeling of familiarity washed over him. He'd heard the tune before, but where?

He played it again. And again. Something was coming back to him ... something...

And then he knew. He knew where he'd heard it.

"*Wait*..." he whispered.

Grace and Kieran gawked at him. "What is it?" asked Kieran.

Arthur darted up from the piano seat and rushed to get his phone. He scrolled along to a *Best of the Best* episode covering the music recital, back when Grace had been following Roddy and Bea.

"I know you're my biggest fan, Arthur, but now's not really the time." Grace winked, referring to when he'd teased her the other day.

"Ha-ha," Arthur grinned. He *loved* the banter he and Grace had these days. Come to think of it, they'd always had banter, only now it wasn't so competitive ... it was just fun.

He took the clip to eight minutes in and hit play.

The same song Arthur had been playing sounded back to them.

Arthur, Kieran and Grace all looked at each other in amazement.

"Who was playing that song?" asked Kieran.

"It was Roddy's little brother, Benjy," Grace answered. "He played the piano for his granddad."

She delved into her bag and unfolded the

music sheet she'd found on the floor outside the FT rooms. The music sheet that had led her to Roddy, with "Lyall" written across the top.

"What if Lyall doesn't mean Roddy Lyall... what if it means *Benjy Lyall*?" said Arthur, voicing exactly what she was thinking. The three of them looked at each other, then back to the note. Kieran turned it over in his hands.

The investigation wasn't over yet.

REUNITED

Standing on the headmistress's front porch, Grace shook her head. How had *she* ended up drawing the short straw? She glared back at Arthur and Kieran, who were hiding behind the bushes at the foot of Ms Lyall's garden.

"You know what this means?" Arthur had said, after they'd worked out that the music sheet belonged to Benjy.

Kieran and Grace waited.

"One of us is invited to Ms Lyall's for tea."

They had all laughed, but that had died down after a few seconds. The idea was scarier than anything they'd done in the investigation so far.

"Looks like it's Boulder, Tree, Axe," Kieran had suggested.

"Is that the same as Rock, Paper, Scissors?" Grace asked.

The boys nodded and they all put their fists behind their backs.

"One … two … three…" Arthur counted.

When they revealed their hands Kieran and Arthur were wiggling their fingers like trees. Grace had hers diagonal like an axe.

"Aha! Scissors beats paper! Axe beats tree.

278

I'm out!" Grace cried.

"Um…" Arthur raised an index finger in the air. "I actually think you'll find axe gets stuck in tree, so tree beats axe. Boulder flattens tree so boulder beats tree. And axe shatters boulder into a thousand pieces *when hit at the right angle…*"

Kieran demonstrated by making a fist then unfurling it slowly in the air, making the sound of a slow-mo explosion.

"…And *that's* Boulder, Tree, Axe."

"That makes no sense. I want a rematch!" Grace shouted.

"Sorry, no rematches. The boulder has spoken."

"But I didn't know the rules! Which, by the way, are completely ridiculous."

"Should've thought of that before you agreed to play." Arthur smirked.

Grace pouted but she knew she'd lost. *She* would be heading into Ms Lyall's house – aka the lion's den – while Kieran and Arthur lurked outside recording. She would be the one to try to get Roddy and Benjy to do a private interview. Because if Ms Lyall caught any of them with a microphone they would all be *dead meat*.

Grace quivered as she stood on Ms Lyall's doorstep. She kept telling herself it was only a house like any other, but somehow it seemed to tower over her like a giant, spooky mansion. A bit like Ms Lyall towered over kids at school. Grace's hand shook as she pressed her finger on the doorbell.

The deep *ding-dong* noise seemed to bellow like Ms Lyall's voice, resounding loudly through the air outside the house. It echoed a few times, getting quieter and quieter, until an eerie silence descended. Then … footsteps.

The door opened a crack and a mop of ginger hair poked out. It was Roddy. And he looked just as terrified to see Grace as Grace was to be there.

"Look, I don't know how you figured it out, but I know why you're here," he hissed. "Can't we do this at school?" He glanced back into the house in fear.

"No, Roddy, it's time to settle this once and for all," Grace said with more bravery than she felt. "It's in there, isn't it? It's in your house?"

Roddy knew! She couldn't believe it… This was confirmation of what they had suspected. How long had he known?! How long had he been covering for his little brother? And the most important question of all… Why had Benjy taken it in the first place? She was itching to interview them!

"Yes, but … please, Grace!" he begged. "My mum will kill me if she finds out!"

That made two of them, thought Grace. She pitied Roddy. The coveted school trophy stolen by the headmistress's youngest son, then covered up by her older son, and hidden in her very own house?! She could only imagine the world of trouble Roddy was going to get in. But as sorry as she felt for him, that wasn't her problem. Good journalism was all about finding the story and keeping it professional.

"Look, Roddy…" she began. But she was cut off by a loud, booming voice.

"Your mother will kill you if she finds out *what*, Roderick?"

Ms Lyall's voice echoed around the hallway. And the porch. And the *street*. Roddy whimpered and the door opened fully to reveal his mum …

… standing in a fluffy, canary-yellow dressing gown.

Grace opened her mouth and closed it again like a goldfish. She wanted to laugh but also cry. It was a strange feeling. From back in the bushes she heard Arthur's voice yelling, "My eyes! My eeeyeees!"

Grace tried to look away but when she cast her gaze downwards she noticed Ms Lyall's matching fluffy slippers with bobbles. She imagined Ms Lyall going to the shops and picking them out. Perhaps fondling the bobbles. How could she ever look Ms Lyall in the eye again? She felt like she now understood the term "emotional trauma".

Despite her attire, Ms Lyall's voice was as cool as ever. "Ms Best, how can we help you?"

"I … uh…" *Keep it cool, keep it cool,* Grace told herself. But all words seemed to have flown out of her head.

"And Mr McLean, Mr Summers," Ms Lyall called to the end of the garden. "You really are the least subtle hiders. And you brought a microphone I see! Jolly good. Why don't the three of you come inside?"

Grace's whole body went cold. This was *not* going to plan. She was supposed to get Roddy and Benjy outside and recover the trophy without Ms Lyall even knowing. Now they were all going inside, Ms Lyall had seen their stolen microphone *and* she was wearing a fluffy dressing gown.

All bets were off. There was nothing else to do but follow her inside.

Arthur had always taken pride in the fact that he was an excellent hider, so Ms Lyall spotting him and Kieran from a good ten metres away had come as quite a personal blow. But there was no time to think about that now. He and Kieran gave each other a solemn fist bump and began shuffling up the front garden towards Ms Lyall's front door. The bushes that lined the path seemed to whisper, "Get awayyyy! You'll never retuuuuuurn!" on the breeze. As they set foot in the house the door slammed shut and Arthur could've sworn no one closed it.

He shuddered. Then he saw Ms Lyall's fluffy bobble slippers sticking out from a chair in the living room and shuddered again for a different reason.

"We're in here," Ms Lyall called.

Arthur and Kieran moved further into the house. There was no escape now.

When they entered the living room Ms Lyall

was sitting up straight in a wing-back armchair, with her hands clasped over her knees. How did she still manage to look totally intimidating in a fluffy yellow dressing gown? Roddy was sitting next to her, looking like he wanted to sink into the floor. An old man that Arthur recognized as Roddy and Benjy's granddad was in the living room, too. As they came in he gave them a friendly wave, although they weren't sure if he remembered them from before.

Grace was opposite Ms Lyall on the other side of the room, trying not to look terrified, but her face was doing tell-tale twitches. Arthur and Kieran sat down either side of her.

"So," Ms Lyall began. "Before we get on to you stealing a microphone despite me confiscating yours, and continuing to investigate despite me forbidding you to do so, let's start with you turning up at my private property and harassing my son Roderick, shall we?"

"Mum, we don't need…"

"Hush, Roderick." Ms Lyall put out a silencing hand and Roddy pressed his lips together. "Well?"

"We, um…" Arthur found his voice was wobbling. He cleared his throat. "We're not actually here to see Roddy, Ms Lyall. We're here to see Benjy."

"Benjamin?" There was a silence and then she began laughing. "My my. I thought it was preposterous enough to accuse Roderick of theft, but *Benjamin?* He's a seven-year-old boy! Goodness, say goodbye to your teenage years, you three, because you'll be in detention until your twenties."

Arthur gulped. He was about to speak again when Roddy interrupted.

"Mum, I…"

"Hush, Roderick."

Roddy pressed his lips together again. His

face turned startlingly red and he looked like he might be about to vomit. "NO!" he shouted. "Listen to me!"

Ms Lyall turned towards him in surprise. Roddy pressed his lips together. You could tell he was half-regretting his moment of bravery already.

"What did you say to me, Roderick," Ms Lyall said. It wasn't a question.

"I ... I said listen, Mum!" He pushed himself off his chair and strode towards the other side of the room where he pulled up a rug.

"Roderick, what on earth are you doing? Sit down this instant!" Ms Lyall called.

But Roddy appeared to be pulling up a floorboard. He put the floorboard to one side and reached down deep under the house, rooting around, covering his arm in cobwebs. Eventually he found what he was looking for and began lifting something up.

Something heavy. Something silver. Something *gleaming*.

It was the trophy.

THE WHOLE STORY

> **GRACE:** "I'm Grace Best at the scene of the most miraculous discovery of the century… Shock is written across the faces of everybody in the room, as the trophy is unearthed… We move to our key witness…"

"Ms Best, turn that microphone OFF!" Ms Lyall bellowed. She looked like a tomato. An angry tomato. An angry tomato in a fluffy yellow dressing gown (not a good look, thought Arthur, although now definitely wasn't the time to mention that). Grace quickly switched it off.

"What is going on, Roderick?!" she fumed. "Get your younger brother down here NOW!"

Roddy finished dusting the trophy off and nodded. He left it sitting on the table as he ran out of the room, presumably to fetch Benjy. They all sat in silence as his footsteps sounded along the hallway and up the stairs. Ms Lyall was breathing heavily. Kieran had opened up a nervous snack of cheese dippers. Roddy and Benjy's granddad, who Arthur had sort of forgotten was in the room, sighed deeply.

It was incredibly tense as they waited. The only sound was Kieran occasionally biting into a dipper. When Roddy returned, he appeared to be alone. Then he moved to one side and revealed Benjy, who was standing close behind him. *Gosh, he really is small,* thought Arthur. How could a boy this small have caused so much havoc? And why?! Roddy held Benjy's hand and both boys went and sat between their mum and granddad.

"Start from the beginning, please," Ms Lyall said. Her tone had softened. Benjy's eyes were like saucers. He looked very scared and upset. You could tell he felt too nervous to explain. He looked towards his brother, who took a deep breath.

"Benjy was sitting in the front row the night of the chess tournament," Roddy began.

Suddenly Arthur remembered seeing him there. Of course! He was with Ms Lyall, right at the front! All the families of the contestants got to sit close to the stage.

"After the lights went out and came back on, he was close enough to see Misha putting her shoes back on."

"I thought it was strange," Benjy piped up.

"Misha Klimach was the original thief," Roddy explained. "I guess she took her shoes off so she wouldn't make a noise."

"Actually, she has a nickel allergy…" Kieran threw in. Ms Lyall glared at him and he stopped talking and ate another dipper.

"Misha Klimach stole the trophy? So why is the trophy *here*?" Ms Lyall demanded.

Roddy explained that Benjy suspected Misha of being the Victory Road thief. He was planning to tell Roddy about it so they could look into it and return the trophy… But when he spoke to Roddy, he realized his big brother was actually *relieved* the trophy had been stolen.

"Relieved?" Ms Lyall frowned. "Why would you be relieved about theft?'"

Roddy sighed and put his head in his hands. His little brother touched him on the arm and they looked at each other. Clearly Roddy had something to say to Ms Lyall, but was too afraid. "I guess…" he said softly. "I guess I didn't really want to be in the chess tournament. And the trophy being gone took everyone's attention off the tournament itself."

Ms Lyall unclasped her hands and went uncharacteristically quiet.

"And…" Roddy went on. "I *really* don't like disappointing you. So when the trophy was taken… Well, you were so focused on the theft that you forgot I'd lost."

Ms Lyall pressed her lips together in a thin line. Roddy's granddad patted him on the back.

Ms Lyall said, "Is that what you think? That I was disappointed in you?"

Roddy shrugged. Ms Lyall sighed deeply. Arthur, Grace and Kieran all averted their eyes. What kind of awkward family situation had they stumbled into? It might've been easier to handle if Ms Lyall was fully clothed.

"I know I put you forward for things, but…" Her eyes darted between her sons and she looked flustered. It was almost more unsettling than the dressing gown. "I've never been disappointed in you, Roderick. I'm so sorry you felt that way. I only want the best for you. You have so much potential. I'm sorry if I've pushed you too hard."

"It's OK, Mum," Roddy said quietly. "I know."

"I hope you know that I'm…" Ms Lyall paused to swallow. "I'm *very* proud of you."

She moved towards her two boys and gave them a long hug. Their granddad smiled over them. Arthur, Kieran and Grace looked at each other. Grace and Arthur thought they'd better wait for the appropriate moment to speak, but then—

"Um," Kieran interrupted through a mouthful of dipper. "Sorry to break up the group hug but how did *Benjy* end up with the trophy? I'm dying to know." He rubbed his hands together as Ms Lyall threw him another glare and sat back down.

"I didn't want everyone to fight over it," said

Benjy, finally gaining the confidence to talk for himself. His cheeks flushed a little red. "The trophy made Roddy feel bad, and it made Misha feel bad too. So I followed Misha to her locker one day, and I saw her locker combination. No one is ever suspicious of me. She didn't even notice me. I'm too small."

Ha! Grace thought. *I knew I'd been right not to underestimate the small and innocent-looking people!* (OK, she had suspected the *wrong* small and innocent-looking person ... but still!)

Benjy looked down at the floor, his cheeks burning with shame.

So it had been *Benjy* that Grace had seen snooping that day, not Roddy! That must have been when he dropped his music sheet, seconds before she turned the corner. Grace felt like such a fool. She'd nearly caught him red-handed!

"I thought I was doing a good thing," Benjy continued, almost in tears. "I stopped everyone fighting and gave the trophy a better home. But I know it was wrong to steal it. I'm really sorry, Mum."

"What were you planning on doing with it, Benjy?" Ms Lyall asked.

"I wanted to give it to granddad," Benjy answered.

Suddenly, every head in the room snapped towards the old man in the corner. He reached a hand out and rested it on Benjy's shoulder. "Oh goodness," he said. "I … I fear I've been the source of much trouble. Yes, Benjy did come to me with the trophy."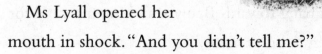

Ms Lyall opened her mouth in shock. "And you didn't tell me?"

"I … I forget. He was going to return it,

weren't you, Benjy?" He shook Benjy's shoulder. Benjy nodded.

"Don't blame granddad, Mum, you know his memory isn't what it used to be. He told me to return it … I know I should have returned it straightaway but … I was scared."

"But … *why?*" Ms Lyall asked.

"Granddad didn't get his medals," Benjy said defiantly, "for everything he did in the war."

There was a stunned silence. Grace, Arthur and Kieran had all heard Mr Lyall's stories, so this was a huge shock. How could he have not been given medals to honour everything he'd done? Their mouths all hung open.

"My name was put forward for a gallantry medal, although I never received any formal recognition," explained Mr Lyall. He faltered, gesturing towards Benjy, searching his mind for his grandson's name.

"Benjy," Ms Lyall said kindly.

"Benjy was just looking out for me, weren't you, pal?" He smiled at his grandson and Arthur noticed his eyes were brimming with tears.

Silence descended upon the room once again. Everyone was lost deep in thought. Suddenly, this was so much bigger than a chess trophy. Grace, Arthur and Kieran sat thinking about all Mr Lyall's stories, about everything he'd done for the country and future generations, some of whom may never have been born if it weren't for him.

"I just wanted Granddad to have something," Benjy mumbled. "He deserves a trophy more than anyone in the entire world."

Up until now Arthur, Kieran and Grace had all been dying to interview the Lyall family – they'd all been picturing the likes, the comments, the praise, the spontaneous applause in the hallways. *The ratings.* But the mood between them had shifted. Now it just didn't seem right. Any of it.

"You should keep it, Mr Lyall," Arthur said.

"Yeah, for real," added Kieran.

"We'll go away and we won't tell a soul," Grace promised.

"Thank you, kids." Mr Lyall's voice was choked up. "But knowing Benjy thinks I deserve it, and that he brought it to me, means more than any trophy. You should return it and get your scoop." He winked.

At that, Benjy's eyes widened again. "Please don't say I'm a thief on Listen Up," he pleaded. "Everyone will hate me!"

"Don't worry, Benjy," Arthur said. "Your secret's safe with us." He looked at Ms Lyall reassuringly. She had been oddly quiet for the last few minutes, and folded her arms across her bright, fluffy dressing gown.

"I suppose things have changed, somewhat," she said eventually.

Grace, Arthur and Kieran shifted towards the

edge of the sofa… Was Ms Lyall going to let them record?

"Do you mean…?" asked Grace.

Ms Lyall huffed. "In light of recent events, I think it only fair to let you record the return of the trophy – *but* …" She waved a stern finger. "You are *never* to break my rules again. And you are *not* to reveal the thief. Do I make myself clear?"

Benjy, Roddy and their granddad looked at them hopefully. Grace, Arthur and Kieran grinned at each other.

"Consider it done, Ms L," said Arthur. "And will you throw in a pair of those slippers to sweeten the deal?"

"Don't push it," said Ms Lyall. But Arthur could've sworn he saw the smallest hint of a smile on her face.

RETURNING
THE TROPHY

[INTRO: *Radio Royalty* jingle (5 secs).
Best of the Best jingle (7 secs).]

GRACE: "Listen Up, Victory Road! We bring you this very special broadcast…"

ARTHUR: "Which not only sees the return of Victory Road's much talked about missing trophy…"

KIERAN: "But sees *Best of the Best* and *Radio Royalty* do their very first…"

GRACE, ARTHUR, KIERAN: "Joint show!"

After they left Ms Lyall's, Arthur, Kieran and

Grace stood outside on the pavement in shock. For at least thirty seconds, no one said a word.

"Well, that was…" began Arthur.

"Interesting," finished Grace.

"Yeah," added Kieran.

They were silent again. Everyone was thinking the same thing, but no one wanted to say it. Until…

"DIBS ON REVEALING THE TROPHY'S BACK!" shouted Arthur, just as Grace shouted,

"DIBS ON COVERING THE TROPHY'S RETURN!"

"I said it first," declared Grace immediately.

"I believe *I* started speaking a millisecond of a millisecond before you did," replied Arthur.

"I am *not* playing Boulder, Tree, Axe again," Grace scoffed.

"Neither are we!" cried Arthur. "This is too important!"

"You both said it at the same time," concluded

Kieran, ever honest and straightforward.

Grace put her hands on her hips. Arthur folded his arms. They faced each other down. They'd both worked so hard to get here, and they knew that keeping Benjy and Misha's secret was the right thing to do, but now covering the return of the trophy was the only way to *not* make this a total loss for their shows.

"I worked out about the slime being Misha's," said Grace.

"If it hadn't been for *me* playing piano, we never would have realized the music sheet was Benjy's," said Arthur.

"If I hadn't—" Grace began.

"Guys, GUYS!" Kieran shouted. Grace and Arthur stopped talking instantly. They had *never* heard Kieran shout before.

"You've both done too much to unpick who did what. We all have! That's why it's called *working together.* Remember when you agreed

304

to do that, yeah?"

Grace and Arthur both looked at their toes, like they were five-year-olds being told off by their parent.

"Don't be doughnuts," Kieran added with a shrug.

Arthur shrugged. He hadn't meant to downplay Bestie's part in the investigation. She had been brilliant. He wouldn't admit it to anyone, but he'd always been a bit intimidated by Grace. She reminded him of his sister Kirsty – pretty much amazing at everything, appearing to stroll through life on a path of A-stars and roses. But in the last few days he'd seen a different side to her. Not *everything* came easily to her. He used to think she was a bit standoffish, but now he saw it was just Grace's defence against people who were only being her friend because of Listen Up. Grace was actually loads of fun once you got to know her.

Grace was also feeling bad. She hadn't meant to take away from the part Arthur played in finding the trophy. Arthur and Kieran had been brilliant. They were so good at drawing important information out of people, and Arthur was crazy creative and more daring than she'd ever have been on her own. Plus ... well, she'd *really* enjoyed working with him and Kieran. For the first time ever it felt like she wasn't on her own, or with people only talking to her because they were trying to get on Listen Up or because they were a fan of *Best of the Best*. Despite her fierce independence she'd found she actually enjoyed ... well ... being part of a team for once. Fighting now would mess all that up. She thought of Mr Lyall and his camaraderie and how much he'd done without any recognition, and she was really making a fuss about giving up *this?*

"You're right," Grace admitted. "Without

you playing that music, we never would have found the trophy. You should break the scoop."

"Nah, *you're* right. If you hadn't worked out that slime was Misha's, we wouldn't even have found the note in the first place. You should do it," Arthur said.

Kieran slapped his palm against his forehead. "You guys really *are* doughnuts. That wasn't what I was saying. Why don't we cover it together?"

Grace and Arthur's foreheads wrinkled in unison. "Together?" Arthur repeated. Two weeks ago, if anyone had suggested doing a joint show with Grace Best he'd have laughed them out the building. But now he was actually considering it.

"Imagine it." Kieran put his arms around both their shoulders. "*Best of the Best* and *Radio Royalty's* loyal listeners combined. All right, so, it's not going to be the scoop we thought it'd be. But we could pull together to make an awesome show, yeah?"

Grace had never, ever imagined sharing air time with anyone, let alone Kieran and Arthur. It still sounded a bit crazy, but…

"What would we call it?" she asked.

"*Queen Bestie and the Kings of Banter.*" Arthur put his hands out in front of him, as if imagining the name on a Broadway sign. "Ooh ooh, *Royal Besties*!"

"Hmm, maybe we don't need a name," said Grace.

Kieran patted Arthur on the shoulder. "I liked it, mate. Anyway, are we agreed?"

A smile curled the corner of Grace's lip. Arthur nodded. "I'm in," he said.

"Me too," agreed Grace.

"Yes!" Kieran punched the air, then put his arms around both of them. "Imaginary glasses in the air please. To our first joint show!"

Grace and Arthur obliged, raising their imaginary glasses to the sky and smiling.

The next morning at school the trophy "mysteriously reappeared" in Ms Lyall's office and Grace, Arthur and Kieran were first on the scene. They did live coverage and posted with a hashtag #thetrophyreturns, which started trending around school within minutes. Before long a huge crowd had gathered outside Ms Lyall's office and no one cared about going to registration … even the teachers! Ms Grant and

Mr Pathak were right at the front of the throng, poking their heads around Ms Lyall's door. Hushed whispers and gasps echoed around the hallway. Everyone wanted to see for themselves but as there was limited space, most people couldn't see a thing and were hanging on to Grace, Arthur and Kieran's every word as they listened to Listen Up on their phones.

You could tell people were surprised to see *Radio Royalty* and *Best of the Best* working together, and they heard a few whispers of, "Is this a joke?" and, "I didn't know Grace and Arthur could even be in the same room without attempting murder," but the news of the trophy soon overtook any whispers about the school radio's most unexpected collaboration.

"And when did you find it, Ms Lyall?" Grace pointed the mic towards their headmistress, now dressed in her usual suit and stiletto heels. Grace smirked, thinking of the fluffy dressing gown.

"It was here when I arrived," answered Ms Lyall. "My door was locked, so I must have left a window open – a mistake I will *not* be making again."

She was good, thought Grace. She sounded as terrifying as ever, and the *last* thing anyone would suspect was that Ms Lyall knew who the thieves were.

"Sneaking into your office in the dead of night ... that's bold, even for the bravest of kids," said Arthur. "Sure it wasn't you, miss?"

At that, the entire school burst into laughter and Arthur winked as Ms Lyall's eyes narrowed. Grace nudged him in the ribs with her elbow.

"I'll be talking to Alan about installing extra security measures around the school," Ms Lyall went on.

"And how did you feel when you saw it?" Grace questioned.

"Stunned, but relieved the trophy is back

in its rightful place. I'm pleased to see that the Victory Road thief had a change of heart."

At that, Arthur glanced over at Misha, who was standing nearby, linking arms with Nikita, then he looked at Roddy standing with his arm around Benjy. He thought of Roddy and Benjy's granddad and his eyes shining with tears over his grandson's affection and pride. The journalist in him was itching to tell the world the whole truth, but he knew in his heart that not outing either of the thieves was the right call.

"To which end, I'm calling off the school's investigation," said Ms Lyall. "Now that the trophy has been returned, it no longer seems important to know the identity of the thief. I want to show the students of Victory Road that they'll be rewarded for doing the right thing."

At this, cheers and whoops echoed through the corridors. Ms Lyall smiled at Grace, Arthur and Kieran, and Arthur noticed her glance affectionately at her sons.

"And what now?" Kieran asked. "Will the trophy stay locked in the cabinet until next year?"

"Oh, I don't know about that," Ms Lyall replied. "I believe we've got a chess tournament final to finish. That is, if Nikita Klimach and Jordan Baptiste will join us for a rematch."

Nikita and Jordan's eyes lit up, and they looked at each other across the crowds as if to say *game on*. And so their rivalry continued. Arthur hoped that one day they might stop competing with each other long enough to actually have a chat. *They might find they've got a lot more in common than they think*, he thought to himself, smiling at Grace as she held out the mic for one last question.

"And Ms Lyall…" Grace said, with a glint in her eye. "If *you* were going to steal a trophy, what would you steal it for?"

Everyone in the hallways stifled a laugh. The thought of Ms Lyall nicking anything was ludicrous. Arthur smiled. He had wondered how their two styles were going to mesh for this joint show, and worried that him and Kieran bantering alongside Grace's blunt questions would seem disjointed and odd. But together they'd *all* done a great job of discussing the trophy's return while also making everyone laugh. They really did make a great team.

"Oh, I don't know," said Ms Lyall. "I've always been rather fond of knitting. Yes, a knitting trophy would be rather glorious."

No one could contain themselves at that, and the hallway rippled with laughter. Even Mr Pathak and Ms Grant grinned at each other.

"Thanks Ms L," said Arthur. "It's been great chatting with you."

The three hosts discussed their relative dream

trophies, aside from journalism (Arthur would be a snowboarding champion, Grace a karate ninja, and Kieran a world-famous eyebrow dancer. Apparently he'd been practising for months), then they closed the show with a promise of interviewing Nikita and Jordan once the real winner of the trophy was finally declared.

As the hallways cleared and Arthur, Kieran and Grace headed back to lessons, Misha caught their eye and gave them a small smile. Benjy waved at them and Roddy mouthed, *thank you* over his shoulder. It wasn't the scoop they had hoped for, but this feeling was better than any sky-high ratings.

FOREVER FRENEMIES

When Arthur and Kieran had first suggested coming round to Grace's on a Wednesday (i.e. Nigerian Night) Grace had felt her chest tighten. She couldn't think of a good excuse fast enough and had panicked and come up with two lame ones instead: washing her dad's car and looking after the neighbour's cat. But she spoke too fast and ended up saying she was "washing her neighbour". In the end, once they'd all stopped laughing, she had to admit about Nigerian Night and how embarrassed she felt about it.

Kieran had blinked in confusion. "Why would you be embarrassed about awesome food?" He had seemed genuinely puzzled.

Eventually she'd agreed to it, but she spent the entire day at school worrying. Now that they were here, joking around with her brothers and chatting to her mum and dad, she finally felt herself relax. Arthur and Kieran seemed genuinely interested in how her mum made the food (and, in Kieran's case, when he could eat the food), and Arthur was telling Grace's parents about how her cooking knowledge had even helped the investigation.

Grace smiled. Arthur was right – all that time spent listening to her mum bang on about Nigerian food – when she had often wished they could just order a pizza – had actually turned out to be a good thing. And in that moment – the smell of her mum's cooking, her family around her, and her friends sitting down to eat dinner with them – she felt a warmth spreading through her.

Arthur was watching Grace from the other side of the room. He hoped she'd feel less embarrassed about being who she was, now. The other day Grace had come over during another Lad Dadz rehearsal and insisted on interviewing the band. Arthur had turned a deep shade of red as his dad had explained the thought process behind their album *Dad Bants,* and key songs like "When Dads Cry" and "Dancing Dad". But Grace had seemed to actually enjoy the music. She even *laughed at one of his dad's jokes*.

After Grace had left, Arthur realized that Grace had helped him feel a little less cringe about his dad and his mates.

"So you're really not going to tell the world about Benjy?" asked Grace's dad, after dinner.

"What about your big scoop?"

Grace inhaled sharply. Her dad had always taught her to go after her dreams. Would he be disappointed in her for letting this one go? She looked at Arthur and Kieran. "Some things are more important," she said quietly.

Her dad's face broke into a grin. He brushed a stray hair out of her face and cupped her chin. "Yes, they are," he said. "I'm so proud of you, Grace."

Grace beamed, flushing with pride, then flinched when she remembered her brothers were in the room. She waited for them to make fun of her.

"We're proud of you too," said Nathan.

"Yeah, good job, little sis," added Lucas. He patted Grace's hair, which was so patronizing, but Grace couldn't help smiling. Were her brothers actually being nice for once?

"We think you made the right choice," Lucas went on.

"We know *Best of the Best* means a lot to you,"

said Nathan. "But sometimes you need to chill. There are other things in life, ya know?"

"I did bet Nathan twenty quid that you were going to sell that little kid down the river, though." Lucas said, nudging Nathan in the ribs. They both burst out laughing and so did everyone else in the room.

"Hey!" called Grace, as they all clutched their bellies.

"Um, sorry Grace." Arthur cleared his throat and tried to stop laughing. "You're just committed, that's all. Nothing wrong with that."

"Nothing wrong at all," her dad agreed.

Grace pouted but she guessed she could understand why they thought that. Maybe a few weeks ago she *would* have outed Benjy to the world, but a lot had happened since then.

As it turned out, not "selling Benjy down the river" had turned out to be the right decision in more than one way. The trophy being returned without anyone knowing exactly who had returned it had got the students of Victory Road talking about the case more than ever. Everyone had their own theories about who did it and how they might have broken into Ms Lyall's office. Everywhere they went someone was discussing their own wacky idea. They'd heard all sorts... The Klimach sisters in bank robber style balaclavas... Roddy Lyall using a machine that cut through the glass of Ms Lyall's trophy case... Tiny Bea Shaffi hiding under Ms Lyall's chair... Jordan Baptiste stuck to Ms Lyall's ceiling, Spider-Man style. There was even a meme going around with a picture of Jordan smirking and a caption that read, "His hair's so big cos it's full of secrets." (When Jordan had seen it he'd laughed until he'd wheezed. Grace thought that was the first time she'd ever seen him smile, let alone guffaw.)

Of course, apart from the Lyalls, only Arthur, Kieran and Grace and their families knew the truth. It had been hard keeping it to themselves, but all the different conspiracy theories and gossiping meant people were replaying *Best's the Best* and *Radio Royalty's* interview clips time after time, trying to work it out for themselves. Their listener numbers were rocketing! And the coverage of the trophy being returned was being shared over and over again. Neither of their shows had ever seen numbers like it – Arthur's sister Kirsty had even told him that she'd seen a group of sixth form girls listening!

When the jollof rice and barbecued chicken was ready, Grace's dad laid the table and her mum began serving. Just as they were about to sit down to eat, Grace saw something on her phone. Her heart started beating faster.

She used to check her ratings obsessively. Weirdly, ever since their coverage had exploded, she'd not been looking as much. The ratings had ended up being less important somewhere along the investigation. But nothing could stop her stomach swooping with delight at what she now saw ... she'd broken her own record for listeners! And if she'd broken hers, she knew Kieran and Arthur had broken theirs too.

"Guys," she said. "Wait. Guess what."

Arthur looked up. Kieran paused, his fork

midway to his mouth. "What? What is it?" he asked over the sound of his own stomach rumbling.

"I think I know," said Arthur. He held up his own phone with a grin on his face. He'd seen it too.

"We broke our records!" they both called out at the same time.

Arthur put his hand on Grace's arm. Kieran's mouth hung open.

"The coverage of the trophy returning has been listened to more times than anything else ever before on *Radio Royalty* or *Best of the Best*!" Arthur went on.

Grace's dad got up and did a little jig and Grace's brothers started cheering.

"Oh my God, Grace, that's amazing!" said Grace's mum, as she got out of her chair and planted a kiss on Grace's head.

Grace, Arthur and Kieran were all in shock.

This was a dream come true! Grace couldn't count the number of times she'd gone to sleep thinking about these kinds of numbers. Arthur thought of all the times he and Kieran had pretended to reach them and bowed to each other, throwing fake roses at each other's feet.

But this was real.

As Arthur and Kieran were leaving, Grace stood outside with them on the front door step. They were all still in a daze.

"Congrats again, everyone," said Kieran.

"Yeah, congrats," agreed Grace.

It was going to take time to sink in. Most tuned in to coverage *ever* on either of their shows! It was going to be hard to top that.

"So, see you tomorrow?" said Kieran.

"Yeah, see you tomorrow," replied Grace. There was silence for a moment, then:

"It's the swimming finals..." Arthur and

Grace said at the same time.

They snapped their heads towards each other.

"What time are you getting there?" asked Arthur.

"What time are *you* getting there?" asked Grace.

"Not sure," said Arthur.

"Me neither," said Grace.

Kieran shuffled back and forth on his toes awkwardly. "We should get going, Arthur—"

"Who are you interviewing first?" said Arthur, interrupting him.

"Who are *you* interviewing first?" Grace replied.

"Not sure," said Arthur.

"Me neither," said Grace.

Kieran rolled his eyes and put his hands up between them like a wrestling referee. "Come on, you've come so far..."

"Done your research?" asked Grace.

"Obviously not," replied Arthur. "Some of us prefer to be *spontaneous.*"

"Spontaneous is just another way of saying *unprepared.*"

They were now standing barely a few centimetres apart with their arms folded. Kieran looked between them in horror. Then they both burst out laughing.

"And there I was thinking that things were going to get boring," Arthur managed to say as he caught his breath.

"Nah, what would I do if I wasn't beating you?" asked Grace.

"Beating me!" cried Arthur. "We *both* made those ratings, Grace."

"And *I'm* going to beat them again … by myself," Grace retorted. She stuck her hand out towards Arthur. "Just because we're friends now doesn't mean I don't want *Best of the Best* to top the ratings every week. We keep our friendship and our rivalry separate, deal?"

Arthur shook Grace's hand. "For ever frenemies."

Grace extended her hand towards Kieran and he shook it too. "What a pair of doughnuts," he muttered, rolling his eyes again.

As Arthur and Kieran walked back along the path Arthur glanced over his shoulder. Just because they were friends now, didn't mean he was going to go easy on her. He wanted *Radio Royalty* to knock their joint record off the charts.

Grace smiled back at Arthur as she waved them off. From now on she was upping her game even more. *Best of the Best* was going to blow *Radio Royalty* out of the water.

Sure, they had done amazingly, but neither of them were going to slow down now. It was breaking their own records today, breaking *school* records tomorrow.

After all, what was a bit of competition between friends?